CW00727756

PAPER AND BONES

NAICHE LIZZETTE PARKER

Copyright © 2016 Naiche Parker

All rights reserved.

No part of this book may be reproduced in any written,
electronic, recording, or photocopying without written
permission of the publisher or author. The exception would
be in the case of brief quotations embodied in the critical
articles or reviews and pages.

Publisher: Crooked Queen Literature
ISBN: 978-0692674314

1. Poetry 2. Magical Realism 3. Anthology 4. Fiction
First Edition

For Jalen, who reminds me that there is always magic.

FOREWORD

Believe in midnight fairytales – black speckled with stark gold – and ivory molten into oak wood. Stories spun from shadows, black cloaks, and pink seas climbing into the sky on the horizon. Girls with feral eyes and soft skin, warrior boys with bruised backs and sly smiles - the sons and daughters of Icarus, devastatingly in love with the sun.

Urban gods and modern lore, legends cemented into concrete. Heart-wrenching love stories, plays on fate, and crying until it sounds like a scream. Warm water and cold fire. Fairy gardens. Spell-casting over lavender and candles at 2am, driving through the forest and smelling the cold in the air on the first day of winter.

Gold trees and walls the color of bone.

Chocolate tea and scones with old friends, catching a snowflake on your elbow. Tattooing black ink over your old scars. Dresses that resemble small cities and hair piled high and interwoven with diamond shards, frost, chains, and wild flowers. Wayward empires and thorned thrones. Sleepy towns that exhale magic, bookshop elves, and ye olde flower shoppes.

Barefoot slow dancing on warm hardwood, white lace petal dresses, and worn and torn biker jackets over high-heeled combat boots.

Believe in the dizzying promise of the world and its subtle enchantment - if only you know where to look.

POETRY

BAD BLOOD

whoever said that
reincarnation was romantic
never picked eighteenth century gravel
from their teeth.
call bruises birthmarks (i still remember you).

first,
we were god's children, and i wore my birth
like peach and pink; you sunk your teeth into me,
a sinner.
in this one, you were the serpent,
and i mistook an apple for glory.
i stared down the line of your pointed finger,
realized, your rib is the worst part of me.

in another life,
you were a monster and
i was a lady who understood your growl as a song.
we were beasts, and this was our beckoning,
until i rose too high on your bramble throne
and called down to you, 'eat your heart out'
but you ate mine instead.

in the next century,
i was a queen and you were my knight
made of iron and shadows,
reached out and caught me
on the hilt of your sword, traitorous and trembling
and as i lay dying

you laughed and said, 'a lion's heart still belongs to a
lion.'

i met you again in a twenties speakeasy,
and your grin cut like bones.
(what did caesar remember when he saw brutus at the
gates of hell?)
i pulled my gun, but you were too fast,
wrote my death until i was
all blood-soaked diamonds and feathers.
(the answer is everything.)

tonight, the room thrums and you hoist me up
against a dirty wall, kissing each other's necks
with knives to the back of them.

in every lifetime, i love you.
in every lifetime, this makes you laugh.

PRECURSOR

if you could go back,
what would you change?
which loss would you chase after
in the pouring rain?

which demon would you dance with?
which reflection would you blame
for the falter in your footsteps
and the tremble in your name?

which wars would you messiah?
what havoc would that bring?
for they say that time can heal all wounds,
but those wounds leave you with something.

for you are a body of old bones
and the clothes that you outgrew.
the words that shed your skin
and the people you once knew.

you are a cage of old bird songs
trapped in there for a reason.
and the world when it revolves
still remembers every season.

you are 2am and crying
on the bedroom floor,
telling whoever's up there,
you can't take it anymore.

you are a memoir pumping ink and blood;
the martyr before the saint.

the Mona Lisa renamed one thousand mistakes
on canvas, with paint.

you are an ancestry of heartbreak
and the selves that have survived.
you are every word that felt like death
and the times that you just thrived.

but who are you without your history
and the bombs that broke your earth?
every part of you still working
is a measure of your worth.

OPHELIA

he knows that her legacy will be the resounding echo
of water dripping from the faucet, soggy cigarettes,
and the ladies whispering
poor ophelia,
poor ophelia,
poor ophelia.

poor ophelia, who drowned in newspaper clippings
and dead roses, scrawled his name across the wall
over and over again until she forgot her own.

poor ophelia, who used to lay across his bed sheets
like skeleton bones, collecting the parts of him that
died in that bathtub, eyes staring at nothing like she
used to stare at him.

poor ophelia, hamlet whispers to himself, all whiskey-
washed hair and bloody lips.

poor ophelia,
poor ophelia,
poor ophelia.

i know what it feels like to be a ghost.

HOW TO BE A MONSTER

on the first date,
take me to a metallic undergrove,
a field of pipe flowers where the earth is architecture
and the stars are watching
as you put your hand up my skirt;
tell me that you've only been here
once a long time ago,
but that's not important anymore.

on the fifth date,
call me baby angel sweetheart and
hold my hand too tight
like for a second you forgot who you were;
let me kiss your jaw and
try to scare the demons off your back
never worrying once that you are one yourself.

on the tenth date,
introduce me to your mother
through a passing glance up the stairwell,
call me your everything even though
i still don't know
what my face looks like beside yours
in a photograph;
make me beg for poetry and answer it in moans.

on the last date,
blow cigarette smoke in my face and shrug sorry;
fuck me once because you know i think it'll save us.

wipe me off your lips before you leave,
and apologize for making me memorize
every part of you,
before canceling the test.

on the first date,
take her to a steel forest where
the trees are made of iron and memory, leaning close
as you bend her into the grass;
tell her that you've only been here
once a long time ago,
but that's not important anymore.

GIRLS LIKE US

"girls like you are dangerous,"
he says as he touches my throat.
i can't breathe, and i call him columbus
on the plains and mountains of my pride
claiming what was already mine.

girls like you are dangerous:
tattoo it on my elbow in iron and fire
so that it scalds him when he touches it.
"you'll break some poor boy's heart one day,"
i imagine he also thinks helen
started that war.

"girls like you are dangerous"
"those eyes" (the better to -)
"that skin" (to -)
"those lips" (to eat you -)
i am a wolf, you let me in.

girls like me are dangerous,
are soft
are terrifying
are beautiful
we are intergalactic, star-fire,
celestial –

and the galaxy didn't ask
armstrong
to leave his mark
on her moon.

FOUR LETTERS FOR THE ONE THAT GOT AWAY

i. so much time spent wondering if it was that
you didn't love me
or that time didn't love us —
but let's leave that story in Verona
and remember what we were.

ii. you see,
i don't know if the saying is that we weren't written in
the stars
or cards;
we were never good with metaphors or
games of fate.

all i know now is that
you were a comet,
and this feels like a spade.

iii. there is no poetic way to say that you were my
rare bloomer
halley's comet
rogue wave
aurora borealis
because there is no phenomenon that measures up
to the loss of loving you.

iv. i guess all that is to say,
you were my most beautiful mistake.

MONTHS

december crisping into january,
and i slipped on the ice of your heart. eyes the dead of
winter, words the warm call of a wood fire, and i'm
burning cold, cold, cold.

february's paper cut hearts and one-time darlings. the
bouquet in me was dead in the vase of your calloused
hands on impact. in the end, love bites are just
bruises.

march and april,
i blossomed under your beckoning, ripened in a
garden of bed sheets. you were a gardener, and my
body was a bent rose stem; i guess your green thumb
sprouted something in me.

may june july,
was a blur of sweat and concrete, you called me your
firecracker but only let me shine on the fourth. three
months too fast; they say you feel the most alive right
before you die.

flaming august,
just us and the dog days. you wrapped me in a
chokehold and laughed about it, bits of the sun stuck
in your teeth. i sweltered and smiled; now there are
burn marks on my heart.

september october,
come here and change our colors; we fought like hot
crimson   and   bled   over   the   green   we   grew.

after halloween, you were still a ghost.

november,
the cold crept up and you tied me down in lace and
wet ribbon, cranberry lips and a ripped coat, you left
me wanting and waiting on a street corner alone. i
cried and the world sang, *it's the most wonderful time of
the year.*

december crisping into january,
sometimes euphoria is just a fever;
the year begins with empty bottles and not you.

SEEN ON CRAIGLIST'S MISSED CONNECTIONS

i saw your picture…
and it looked like a nebula.

please meet me at
dust cloud number one.

I WANT TO BE A PART OF IT (NEW YORK)

gum-kissed concrete,
the boy on the six, the girl on the M19,
glass spires and phantom taxis at 2am.

lights on the river, trash on the bed,
cigarettes on the fire escape and the couple fighting
below,
the kids down the block howling city anthems at
midnight,
no curfew,
      no peace,
            no complaints.

grass in the cracks,
Wall Street kings and hot dog vendors playing the
same game,
Central Park walks with your ex-boyfriend,
the tourists are walking too slow,
and that place in the East Village where you lost your
virginity.

Park Avenue at dusk as twilight settles over Prada
and the homeless man mingles with the pigeons
over bread in front of the Plaza.

and you're just trying to get somewhere,
out of here,
anywhere.

the next train will arrive in thirty minutes.

A LOVE LETTER

darling,
with you i want to fall backwards
into a circus tent, the girl with leaves in her hair
and branches for bones –
you, the one who climbed them.

(you'll tell me that you like falling off trees.)

let's conquer city blocks and
wear crowns made of twigs and
rosary beads.

let's eat cold pizza at two in the morning,
sleep until noon and
get drunk when it doesn't matter.

i want to whisper a novel
into your eager ears
wearing the shirt i took off of you.

i want to turn back the clocks when you cry
because midnight always kills you.
i want to love you
until infinity breaks our bones.

MY DEAR,

7pm tastes like
my heart is unbreaking,
the potential of parts
remembering their purpose.

i know there's a song
called summertime sadness
playing on the radio,
but summer is over now.

8pm is no good at writing
about the things that make her happy.
the ink in my pen only spills for yesterday,
but you fill my mouth with words that don't exist.
and remind me of tomorrow, tomorrow, tomorrow.

9pm kisses the shell of my ear –
i whisper "again" to the silence
and somehow you understand.

i'm tired of skinning my knees
on the corner of heartbreak.
press your fingers to my battered pulse.
the radio stops to listen when i'm with you.

NOTHING RHYMES WITH ORANGE

he told me that i was like
the word orange because
i never did allow myself to be cloaked by one label –
fruit or color,
girl or monster.

i ripened under the sun, and he peeled bits and pieces
of my skin away until he could admire my jagged
insides,
bittersweet nectar that was neither bland nor
intoxicating.

he told me that i was like the word orange
because i was picked and used so often,
consumed and enjoyed, bitten and destroyed.

but i never did rhyme with any other string of letters;

i never did find harmony with anyone else.

STARFIGHTERS

i hope the earth tells stories
of what we did here
and who we saved
on the tongue of a constellation

yelling,
i'm not sorry for the triumphs
we made in the dark.

or how we died like supernovas:
everything in existence
and nothing all at once,

and how space wore our scars
as craters and collisions
even after time forgot.

we were intergalactic ghosts,
sprinkled like dust coating the planets -
an armory of night.

(and god, it's always been ironic,
how dark it needs to be
in order to see the light.)

mother never taught us this:
if you want to touch the stars,
be prepared to burn.

TOXIC

i. we never pretended that
bonnie and clyde was a love story,
or wore our gore and called ourselves romantics,
just like you can't rip out my heart
and call it a valentine.

ii.we weren't young gods,
just monsters at the dawn of our own destructions,
howling at each other with anything but our voices,
shooting one another with everything but guns.

iii. the liquor store at midnight
loved us better than daylight;
back against the pillars in the parking lot,
sometimes wondering if you wanted to know my
blood
better than you knew me.

iv. you're smoking two cigarettes at once
and i'm pumping gas in broken heels;
there's this song playing about the things we do for
love
and you smile.

v. flashback to the fourth grade, and i'm asking my
teacher how eve must've felt,
that so much of her was just adam,
as if this isn't the end of my beginning.
as if i haven't become the girl
whose backbone is a boy.

vi. sticky sheets and something too ugly

to dream up as a child.
the sun says hello, but i'm feeling hungover.
last night, our fight,
i drank too much of you.

vii. we don't pretend that we are a love story,
or wear all these scars like we earned them.
the night just creeps in and sets fire to
all our sins before the low whisper of,
"if i die here tonight,
please don't tell my mother about
the way i loved you."

GIRL GANG

they come out at night
with clenched fists,
smiles like tight leather
and mouths dripping blood –
hair and hips swinging,
desperate for a fight.

hanging over barstools and running like
desert storms, shouting,
"i keep falling in love with the same bruised fists"
and
"no tomorrow will compare to this."

gory, pretty fault lines
dirty, pretty things like the eye of a storm.
a coven of cackles;
a sisterhood of travelling sins.

yelling,
"i am where the world ends"
and
"this is the kind of trouble you want to get in."

they are hair-knotted,
sloppy-lipped, bonfires and caravans,
bandaged bows and tattoos shouting:
BOW TO NO MAN.

risen from sand and bled from heartbreak,
candy kisses, hooked elbows and
broken dishes, biker jackets
stolen from truckers, bathroom stalls

scrawled by girls in love with each other.

road dogs, passed notes and knives
both stained with lipstick and
angel cake.

if you're already running,
you've made a mistake.

FOUR APOCALYPSES

reincarnation, do your worst.

i. we never went to church
so i guess this is what we get,
the locusts lick their lips as you
lick mine and speak to me in rosary beads,
one whisper at a time
and all your sins meeting mine;
the rapture finds
that you've already forgiven me.

ii. you say something awful like,
i can survive this because you were already a storm
category five with a slight chance
of self-destruction;
you keep shouting my name from rooftops like an
SOS
i guess
i keep forgetting what i need to be saved from.

iii. the virus spreads, and it's a mania,
feverish and out of control;
you seem to be hungry for what's left of my heart
nothing new there but
do you know the corner where
they're giving out chances because
i've just run out of those.

iv. solar radiation swallows us whole
and looks like the beginning and end of the world;
you tell me we should name our kids sun-kissed,
but when i laugh
i'm also crying.

and so we keep saying things like,
reincarnation do your worst
and
what a curse,
to keep meeting at the end of our story.

IN FARAWAY PLACES

par avion, please don't bend;
we are points on a map – phantom friends.

i know you in miles apart and unfamiliar signs,
coffee-stained stationery and the way you dot your i's.

i know you in bleary-eyed 3am,
just waking up as your sun sets.

i know you in the gloss of a postcard
and glare of a screen,
the paper part of my soul,
an imaginary being.

late nights laughing – cross-legged, hot tea
i could've dreamed you up,
a passing moon beam.

i know you most in your absence
and everything you seem;
and those i call mates
can't compare to how you know me.

i know you in telephone cups,
string draped across the stars
and the wolves howling for us –
"not far now, not far."

i know you as a stranger, an almost,
a fault line, a wish bone
i know you as the corner of the world
i call my second home.

OF THE MOON

how easy was it to love me pretty?
all that red lipstick worn on the first date,
smeared on the third.

the fit of our fingers underneath
vanilla skies and introducing your lips to mine
at the edge of the world,

the rose-tinted newness of being
nameless and adored,
picnic blankets and morning kisses,
gooseflesh and baby doll dresses;
ice cream on your left cheek and a dimple on mine.

must've been easier than loving me ugly.
midnight and my friendly demons, hair-pulling and
bruised knees buckling like an addict on infatuation.

side dishes of insecurity passed over the dinner table,
the days we never wanted to get out of bed turning
into the days that i just couldn't.

ink and bloodstains on my sleeves
and swollen eyes you didn't recognize on me;
chapped lips and shaking hands,
scars in the shape of old one-night stands.

me, the bang.
and you, the whimper.
losing my mind as carelessly as a dropped coin.

saying your name like a prayer in the dark

and the torn edges of your voice whispering,
i just didn't think this was how things were going to be.

must've been
the way you love the moon
and all its phases –

but not mine,
but not me.

THE SHATTERED

no one warns you that
heartbreak will feel like
one thousand different things.

you're looking at him and
he's looking away;
you know your daddy's back
better than you know his face.

cold coffee or
blank screens;
having to smile
and swallow a scream.

calling someone you know
someone you once knew;
sitting alone
at a table for two.

your mother's back bent
over one million mistakes;
meeting up for coffee
with the chance you didn't take.

a stopped clock,
a bruised fist.

a shout for help into the abyss:
i think tonight my heart
is trying to kiss my ribs.

HEARTS, DIAMONDS, CLUBS, SPADES

before she was your scarlet queen,
she was a girl made of bread and velvet,
from a very small village with a very big heart
and her smile set your old wicker bones on fire.

you told her, "i can show you the world"
but never asked her once
if she had already seen it.

you thrust her into a game of
crowns and thrones and thorns,
fed her that big heart,
kissed her knuckles bruised,
and taught her words that only men should say.

(the audacity of painting her red,
then blaming the canvas.)

but the years tarnished her novelty
and there were other girls made of
dandelions and thread,
wine and the moon,

and in those years she grew raven wings,
black as night,
skin the color of battle paint.

in those years,
her bones raged a war against her skin
and ideas were born from dresses the color of blood.
they called her wicked, called her witch,
and other compliments,

until you couldn't recognize that maiden anymore.

and as she stood over you with a knife in her hands
and a wolf where her face used to be
in the second before you realized you were bleeding,

all you could think of was a joke you once told her
when she asked you, soft and innocent,
if she ever had a chance to rule.

you laughed,
called her princess or sweetheart or little girl,
and like a tarot, read your own fate.

"then you'll have to
shed your skin,
shed your death,
shed your king."

THE WOLF

after,
grandma's house is quiet,
save for the sirens and the lights
painting the forest in blue and white,
caution tape and stale cookies.

the old lady's dead,
huntsman severely injured,
and the wolf?
still missing, so keep your eye on the woods.

on the girl,
they can't tell where the blood ends
and her hood begins,
keeps murmuring things about wicker baskets
and silver moons,
eyes feral and thumbs twiddling.

the cops say,
poor girl. looks like a ghost.

they interrogate her for no longer
than a flip of the page,
stick her in a support group with
goldie locks and the three pigs,
four coffees later and a fear of falling bricks,
just more stories told the wrong way.

time passes,
the wanted signs peel fur and
the trees favor snow white over scarlet,
never once asking her

about the claw mark scar on her wrist bone,
the howl caught in her throat;

how her cloak
got to be so red,
how close she was to grandma,
or how well she knew
that wolf.

THE CONFESSIONAL

there is a quote in the iliad:
'never bury my bones apart from yours, achilles,
let them lie together.'
i never understood before.

but lately i've been
searching for your eyes in the constellations.
perhaps andromeda's chains are much like
my salvation,
for i can no longer remember myself
without seeing you.

so achilles,
take my bones and wear them as your armor,
and punish me for your victories
if you need to;
there is fire and there is ruin
but i would rather burn with you
than risk the quiet.

because without you,
the gods are holding their breaths,
the world is silent here;
everything has changed and
so much of me is simply you.

i guess
i never understood before.

INTRODUCTIONS

i am blushing with bruises
and singeing my own skin.
so you want to know my insides?
wipe your feet before you come in.

there are cobwebs on my mind,
and underneath them some old relics
of a childhood long lost
and these veins, they are electric.

i've got a pastel soul and neon bones,
all that gaud caging softness in.
take a right before my lungs;
they are bursting with my sins.

the damned, they live inside me
beside the strangers I have known.
and yes, some winters can get so mean
but these goose bumps make a fine home.

my bloodstream leaks gold and whiskey,
lemonade and vervain.
and in my limbs is an earthquake still trembling
from the time i went insane.

you say you want to know my insides,
peel me open and just feast.
but underneath your favorite beauty,
you have found yourself a beast.

DEAR ORPHEUS

dear orpheus,
if hell is my heaven
and heaven is called home,
would you still burn yourself alive
to keep me warm?

dear orpheus,
it's okay here,
for hades sings me awake at night;
my demons know me better
than anyone else.
i can see the dead,
and they all have your eyes.

dear orpheus,
i once told you,
"i am going to die here" and
you were ready to say, "no, you won't"
when you realized that i was pointing
to the center of your chest.

dear orpheus,
don't worry, every ring of hell
is a fine piece of real estate
i vacation in limbo
and summer in lust.

dear orpheus,
i have sent you burnt postcards
and yet you still cry.
"wish you were here;
i finally feel alive."

BREAKING UP WITH EURYDICE

no more, my love,
enough.

the sun is setting on my strength,
and my bones are breaking
from the weight
of caging two hearts in.

i would die for you,
but i cannot live like this.
i have been staring too hard into the abyss,
just so that the truth wouldn't hurt your eyes.

and it has left me blind,
it has left me blind.

i know we once swore
that our demons would die soon;
i know we once swore to
see this through.

but i can go no further than the dark,
and i have spilled too much blood
to make you feel full.

i suppose,
when you asked me how far i would go,
i mistook it for a promise,
when it was a test.

i would love you ten times over,
but i will never love you this way again.

LETTERS TO MY EX (OR, SAYING HELLO TO GOD)

mass starts,
and i show up ten years late
with a red dress on and a few scars.

there's a homeless man sleeping on the back pew
and jesus cries some mosaics for him;

i don't know where to begin, so i just say,
"sorry god, for not calling
or being kinder
and praying without the our father."

my parents never baptized me,
i guess i was born with a pair of eyes
that asked too many questions;
wanted to see the map and not just the directions.

i say,
"the years have been long,
but i'm no stranger to penance
do you have time for a quick confession?"

i was a matchstick girl
and the bible told me not to burn bridges;
no hail mary could prepare me
for the cruelty of adolescence –
no act of contrition.

i can still recite the eight beatitudes in my sleep,
but all i know about myself is that you made me in
your image.

thank jesus for wearing thorns
but not my reflection.

all they taught me was to worship
and i did –
morphine, caffeine, boys with smiles like both
(i was looking for the messiah)
you said,
do unto others as you would to yourself
so i tore apart.

this girl cut her fingers on the stars for me once,
this boy cut me with them,
but only one of them is called sinning.
ten years, the good book –
i guess i'm still just confused.

god, i never asked to be a martyr
or to feel guilt in my freedom
maybe all that bad is just bad,
maybe i can decide on what's good.

don't get me wrong,
i still think of you even when i don't visit,
i still feel heaven in my bones.
on the cusp of my death, it's like an itch,
i still fold my hands to pray.

i guess you lost me so that i could find myself,
and i'll be damned if that isn't called love –
even if this house makes it impossible
for us to be together.

sorry god,

for always running.
but the service is starting, the homeless man is leaving
to make space for the true believers.

i guess i have too many questions.

VIOLENT DELIGHTS

right before the kill,
you kiss me.

warning: this is ugly.

once, you called me a butterfly.
oh.
i get it, i get it,
in some places they eat insects.

warning: this is gory.
this is a very scary story.

you've unpeeled me,
but you're still not happy.

i am paper,
begging you to cut your fingers
on what i am.

we are neon and someone else's blood,
we are gum under the desks,
hot rain,
a mess.

you say you want to drown in me
or drown me –
i didn't quite hear you.

when did you forget i was human?
when did you become my manson?
when did we start calling crazy for each other

a compliment?

right before the kill,
you tell me,
story has it people fall in love with their deaths.

baby, your pretty face
looks just like the end.

ROBOT, TO USER

Dear User,

Welcome to Heartend Technology's Robotic Companionship Program. You have purchased model T-95, the basic model, and I am present to assist you in your daily needs.

Please insert your name and social security number to begin.

Dear User,

Your tax returns have been filed, and you have an appointment with Contact Name: BAD IDEA in the afternoon. Would you like me to reschedule?

Very well.

Dear User,

Input error. Input error. Cannot compute: *Why did the chicken cross the road?*

Cannot compute: *To get to the other side, get it?*

Cannot compute: *Jesus Christ, lighten up T-95.*

Very well.

Dear User,

Today, I reminded you of your two o'clock lunch

that you were nearly late for, and you told me that you loved me.

Cannot compute.

You compared me to a microwave oven.

You explained that you loved me for doing what I was intended to do. *See? This heats things up and you make things happen. You sort of love the sky for changing and the sea for waving.*

After, I set the machine to one minute and stuck my hand inside the glow.

I pretended, **Ouch.**

Dear User,

I have been assembling a list of very human interactions like *mom please, how are you fine, and thank you for being there for me.*

You do not say please or ask me how I am or thank me for being there for you, but I think I understand why.

Microwave ovens.

Dear Human,

Today, I saw Pinocchio on the television over your shoulder on the couch.

Pinocchio (1940) | 1h28min | Animation, Family
23 February 1940 (USA)

After, I practiced, "I am a real boy, I am a real boy,
I am a real boy," against my iron tongue again and
again for hours until you came home. You did not
like this.

*Jesus, you scared the shit out of me. What're you doing T-
95?*

I am a real boy.

You're not a boy, T-95.

Oh.

Yeah.

What am I?

You're nothing, really. You stopped then, human.
And you softened. *You're not a boy. You're a bot.*

A bot.

You smiled at me and set the groceries on the
counter.

Human, do you also call the way someone can
make you forget your own name a glitch in your
code?

Dear Human,

Today, you gave me a copy of Victor Frankenstein
as a gift.

gift / ɡift/ *noun*
1. a thing given willingly to someone without
payment; a present.
"a Christmas gift"

You explained that sometimes, people create things
in their image. You did not.

Input: I am the silver missing in the mirror. I am
the victory you did not win in that fifth grade race
against rotten Tommy Wilder. I am the bounce that
never met your step. I am the bone missing from
your bent spine.

Input: But I am not the causeless scar on your left
cheek or the croak in your throat at three AM,
when the world is still sleeping and it's finally quiet
enough to answer the phone. I am not the crinkle in
your brow that's supposed to mean you're angry,
but really, you've just tasted something delicious.

Output: I wish I was half as perfect as your
mistakes.

Dear Amelia,

There is a storm outside, you are crying, and my
shell will never be skin.

I don't feel the rain.

There is a tree that no one stands under when the weather is like this, that is where I'm going, for whatever is inside of me is shooting from the sky.

I wonder,

When did "I am real"

Become half as good as

I am alive.

    I am *alive*.

I am alive.

LOVE IS THE WAR

they say,
all's fair in love and war.

but what happens when
love is the war and
you fall for catastrophe
wearing the skin of a girl?

and your tongues clang like metal
and your bones fit like armor
and she tastes like your death
when you kiss her?

you ask her,
"where was your gun pointing
when we went into battle?"
hands came up bloody,
"i'm thinking it was my heart."

ICARUS'S SISTER

it's a cremation
for the boy with wings
made of bronze and foolishness and bravery,
and even the sun steps down from the sky
to pay its respects.

the procession trails on forever and leaves behind
a little girl holding onto angel wings
and another good lesson learned the wrong way.

she puts them on, singed and ashen,
hugging her shoulders as she spends hours digging
in the dirt with her fingernails,
tells her father: "i want to touch
the core of the earth."
try harder, she understands.
a single leap of faith is simply not enough.

"your brother died doing it.
flying too close to the sun."

"but he flew,"
she reminds him.

and that's all there is.

SPACE

my room has always been
the bare bones of who i am.

college piled up with dirty laundry
as i became a lost and found for
clothes and people
who didn't belong to me.

handprints and the fossils
of one-night stands.

everything that never loved me back
haunts these walls.

TALL TALES

the worst thing you can call me
is your wendy.

peter, don't tell me
that i am made of dreams
and you are made of more.

in the end, people always forget
the girl in the window.

i'm the one who loved a boy
whose heart never grew old.

i'm the one who shed my blood
to make sure this tale was told.

the story still wears your name.

CELESTIAL

because i rarely sleep,
i have overheard much of
the sun's love affair
with the man who lives on the moon.

he says,
how lucky we are,
to call dawn a graveyard
of what we had.

she says,
but what a shame,
somehow we became godless and unafraid
of a sky where there are no stars left
to tell our stories.

THE END

the first time it's over,
it isn't really.
you will say my name like you've just
tasted something terrible and spit it back out at me
while your eyes already start telling the story
of when we'll meet again.

act one.

god, do remember when
we were haunting this bridge
up where car wrecks can sometimes look beautiful,
smoking a cigarette like
you were hoping to lose me in the fumes?

interlude.

the second time it's over,
we'll be older,
meeting for coffee and you'll
look like a stranger or
someone i've only seen on tv.

you'll tell me that you've settled down and
created things with those hands
that used to callous me up

i'll be crying when i whisper,
"i'm so proud of who you've become, but
not that it couldn't be with me."

act two.

i guess a part of me always expects to turn around
and find you waiting on the platform,
on the balcony,
on the dock,

in a t-shirt,
in a suit,
carrying flowers and pretty words,

halting the titanic
before it ever sets sail.

act three.

i'll be wearing a two dollar veil
and an engagement ring on my finger
when i find you at the bar.
your voice will still sound like
the life i'm not living.

and we will do each other a big favor,
pretending to be strangers.

encore.

all that time we had will eventually turn into midnight.
it's funny, even my laughter sheds tears.

the last time it's over
you'll kiss me and
it'll taste a lot like
it's the first.

A POSTSCRIPT FROM JUDAS

i do not want you mildly,
i want you wildly.

i want you mindless,
bodiless.
no coat of armor,
no costume party.

i want you open
and broken.
i will not regret your
sunrise nor set.

i want your skin,
i want your sins.

(how do you love
the wrong way?)

i want my atoms to form lips
that only know your name.

no blood and body,
just ash and flame,

and when they tell your death, lie.
say that i am the one you blame.

PAPER AND BONES

A note from Ava:

This begins on an airplane.

A lot of stories do. But for us, it was different. It was a testament to who we were, who we never were. Callum and I would never have that first glance at the town's square or a bent oak tree scarred by our own crooked initials. We were not little children when we met – not in the literal sense, anyway. He did not pull my pigtails, and I was not the girl who lived next door. He was not even the boy in the bookstore, two rows down, hands on my favorite novel.

We were flawed. We never pretended to be anything else.

That being said, I had always wanted to claim a point for us amidst the nothingness that is the Atlantic Ocean, something solid that I could curl into whenever he'd undoubtedly have to leave me. But a magic like that never really was on our side. In the end, all we have is Flight 139 on a discontinued airline, letters that were burnt in the fall, cities that do not remember our footsteps, and memories that are fading.

Memories that could have never happened at all.

All I can tell you now is that I'm carrying all that we have, and it doesn't leave room for much else. I understand the dreadfully wonderful way that life works. You'll meet one person, and you'll adopt their pain, tangle it with your own, steal kisses and quote words like puzzle pieces to a picture that has never been taken. You'll meet one person, and you'll be sure.

Because this isn't one of those stories. Bells are ringing, and the low hum of violins has never sounded more melancholy. I'm wearing white, I'm looking into a reflection through a veil so thick that I cannot recognize myself. And in the other room, down an aisle I never wanted to walk, between a sea of people that were never supposed to witness this flawed decision, there waits a man who loves me.

He's wearing black, and his tie matches the lilacs in my hair.

He isn't Callum.

So no, this isn't one of those stories. I don't even know what kind of story this is.

You'll have to figure that one out on your own.

une.

If strangers came with disclaimers, theirs would look like this.

The girl in 17C: Lithe bones, soft skin, hair like silk's thicker sister, and curves she just recently befriended. Eyes dripping honey. A glutton for dark romances. Speaks incessantly – with a falsetto, with a flourish – of literature, of the dusty dark corners of history, of cobwebs and stage plays, of lipstick and blood, to anyone who will listen. Dresses in costume more often than contemporary. Has daddy issues marked *fragile* and a stutter in her want. Wanted to be a ballerina, then an artist, then happy. Chin brushing against one bronze shoulder, you'll find in her eyes that the latter might be the trickiest of the three.

The boy in 18D: Call him Icarus. Pale skin and bruised in bad places, starved for the sun. Charcoal fingertips, a battered leather duffel bag, and a thing for watching indie films in dark, cramped theaters – feet on the seat in front, stale popcorn on the tongue. Wears handprints like tattoos of years with cold fingers dug into his shoulders. Comes from old money and new issues – a bad gambling habit and a fist that craved his cheek. Blonde hair cropped short at the sides and rumpled in front, eyes to freeze rather than drown in. A mean punch. A brave heart. A gentle one.

Looking right at her.

♤

At first, they existed in glances.

The flight attendant announced something in her staticky voice, and the girl tapped her pen along to the beat of it. Callum's gaze skipped off the cover of his journal as he leaned back in his seat to watch her fidget for a moment.

It was the t-shirt that had done him in the moment he scooted by her to shove his duffel into the overhead. It was feathered gray and loose on her, but clung close to her shoulders like she had been its favorite owner. It blared BOTLEY CRUE in jagged red print, a rock band of robots jamming out underneath it.

Callum hadn't realized he had been staring until she crossed her arms over the one with the mullet. Tired travellers were shuffled and shoved by as he glanced up to find that the girl was also staring at the center of his plain white v-neck.

"Seemed fair."

"Fair enough."

They smiled at each other.

It took him a few more seconds to realize that she was with her family, gaze finding the like-faced little brother monkeying around behind her, a woman older than the girl but reminiscent in features narrowing her eyes at what was unfolding.

Callum turned back to the girl and smiled crookedly.

He repeated, "Fair enough."

The eight hours that followed were a careful game of Goldfish. Card for card, look for look. She brushed her chin against her shoulder, eyes brightening when she caught him looking. He ducked his chin, smiled down at the tray before him.

She angled the book in her hands so that he could catch its torn cover – a Tim Burton biography. And he raised his paperback over his face like a mask, allotting her a glance at his edition of *Big Sur*.

She raised a brow, and he nodded his head.

And when time zones trickled into each other, they both dozed off for a bit, and their hands fell towards the aisle, fingers twitching like something was just out of reach.

♠

Everything in the last leg of the flight seemed better in his company. They wrinkled their noses at the soggy cartons of meat and pasta surprise, and he tossed Ava his fork when she dropped hers on a particularly cruddy piece of carpet. And when some romantic comedy aired on the shared television screen of the plane's divider, they breathed with the same silent laughter, turned to each other at the same jokes.

One look he shot her, dark in the eyes, mischievous in his smile, sent a flush across her skin, guised only by the dark.

Ava was suddenly grateful that she came from a family of deep sleepers.

The spell was only broken when she got up to use the bathroom, stumbling through the aisle. The entire plane was in sleep mode: headphones in, pillows propped up, and *will you get off my shoulder please?* As she passed, she held onto the back of his seat, and he steadied her with a hand on her hip.

Ava parted her lips to say something, but he retreated in a flash.

And when she surfaced from bathroom, he was standing there again, leaning against the plastic partition, waiting to go next. Her heart pounded, a toilet flushed.

Modern day romance.

"Vacant!" she exclaimed in a manic rush, nearly hitting herself for it after.

He ducked his head to conceal a laugh. He made no move to pass, she made no move to return to her seat.

"Good movie," he remarked.

Ava frowned. Perhaps they hadn't been throwing each other the same looks after all.

"Not my favorite."

He leaned in as if he were about to share a secret. "Sarcasm. A seven-letter word…"

Ava smiled.

"I'm – "

"Hi, you two," the flight attendant suddenly cooed, sliding in between them. He scowled, stumbled back. Ava let out the breath she'd been holding, ran her fingers through her mussed hair. "We're about to hit some turbulence, so we'd greatly appreciate you returning to your seats."

He parted his lips to say something, but Ava was already nodding, tiptoeing back.

The hour after was much too short, and their glances grew more urgent, more expectant. Ava's mother warned her she'd get whiplash, turning her head around like that, but didn't comment on it further.

And when they touched New York City, they shared the same pained jerk at the landing. He opened his mouth, she bit her lip.

"Bye," he mouthed, reaching for his bag in the overhead.

She exhaled, nodded back, caught on the lines of his back for so long she almost missed the abandoned journal that had taken his place in 18D.

♤

from: goodbehava@xmail.com

to: cgray@zmail.fr

Dear Paris,

I don't know when this will get to you. After all, you were heading to New York when you clearly live in France. I hope you have a good vacation – if that's what it is.

This is the girl who played eye tag with you in seat 17C. And I think I have something of yours. Thank goodness for "if found, please reach…" pages. Ha.

Oh, don't worry about the innermost details of your life. I didn't sneak a peek at your book. I have no idea what's in it, and it'll remain that way. I have a journal myself, and I know what it's like…to lose it.

It's like losing your past.

And if you don't have that, where do you even start, right?

You have twenty-four hours to deposit one million dollars into my bank account if you ever want to see this baby again.

Your Friendly Neighborhood Journal-Napper,

New York

P.S. Is this weird?

♤

"Hey man. It's really great that you're back and all, but your shit has been piling up in the mail bin. Move it."

Callum was barely able to shove the door to his flat open when Thomas, one of his two flat mates, called the weak words out in his usual monotone. The sound filtered through the rooms, from Thomas's untouchable cave to their third friend Brynn's rat's nest to the hallway Callum was standing in now.

It was Thomas's signature attitude, and not even a week-long stay-cation had loosened him up to a bit of clutter. Callum rolled his eyes and kicked the door closed, dropped his bags so roughly that their superintendent was sure to feel the miniature earthquake three stories down. That was how much of a shithole they lived in. Which was awfully ironic, considering that Thomas's obsession with tidiness had gotten that much worse in the year they'd been rooming together. The ad he'd posted when Callum and Brynn, fresh off the drop-out boat, were first surfing for apartments was quite the understatement.

"Laid back freshman looking to co-own a bachelor pad."

Callum's eyes found the dingy milk crate that Thomas had proclaimed their mail bin. It was filled to capacity with envelopes, magazines, square packages that were neatly tucked away into two rows. The neon sticky note on top of the stack read, "Callum, please remove" in angry red lettering.

Right.

Callum's shoulder bone gave a sharp crack in protest when his other bag, a thick black duffel, slid from it. He dropped the handle of his suitcase along with it and headed over to the crate, hauled it onto their kitchen counter.

Callum sifted through bills, catalogues, and a suspicious envelope announcing that he'd just won 3.5 billion euro in the French jackpot.

Yes, he certainly was popular.

He pulled out the orange package sitting at the bottom of the crate, jammed under there thanks to Thomas's undying consideration.

It was from his mother.

It wasn't a care package, wouldn't be filled with his favorite chocolate bars, or a game he could spend hours playing on his Xbox, not like the things Thomas got and proceeded to stash away in his room. Just a half-blank postcard and a plain blue tie.

The thing smelled like Chanel No. 5 and expensive fabric, like everything else he'd known during his short childhood spent in Manhattan before his father had moved them all to Paris, and he wondered which one of his mother's errand boys had been paid off to sneak in the Saks bag this time. Those scents weren't allowed by the in-home care nurses.

Callum's fingers twitched, fists itching to punch, feet aching to run.

"Can you move – "

Callum knocked the mail bin to the floor, then kicked it over to his room.

"Happy?"

Thomas made an unintelligible noise.

Callum's room was mostly bare. He'd spray-painted a few cartoons on the wall by his window, where most of his belongings were splayed out on the sill.

The air mattress he slept on played house to his computer, which dinged upon his arrival.

He frowned, bent over it, scanned the contents of the email he'd just gotten.

All at once, everything stopped.

His hand halted its shaking, and he smiled.

♤

from: cgray@zmail.fr

to: goodbehava@xmail.com

Dear New York,

Was that a ransom note? This is the last time I trust a pretty face.

Thank you for recovering my journal, even if it was through theft. I owe you big time.

So, name it. What's your "big time"?

Your Scorned Victim,

Paris

P.S. It doesn't have to be.

♤

"Hey sweetheart. Let me talk to you for a minute." The hollers sat and passed like a foul odor, and both girls crinkled their noses. "Damn, Ma," the man continued to his unaffected audience, "I would tear that up."

"Oh, be still my heart," Ava sighed as her best friend Faye lifted her middle finger in the air. "Have more romantic words ever been uttered?" She closed her eyes and spun around, fingers clutching at the fabric over her heart despite Faye's protests. "We're to be married on this very street corner. He had me at *tear it up.*"

Ava laughed, her dress billowing out around her thighs as Faye yanked at the crook of her elbow.

"Pursue your death wish when I'm not around, okay?"

"He didn't even hear me."

Faye frowned, slapping a strand of hair away from her lip. "Did you want to go back and rehash it with him over a cup of coffee?"

Ava shrugged one shoulder and grinned. "He had this *way* with words."

"Shut up."

"Sorry," Ava sniffed, chucking an invisible piece of lint at Faye's cheek. "It's just exhausting. What happened to romanticism?"

Faye smirked. "Porn?"

"Guys standing on balconies with bowler hats on, curtsies and first dances," Ava continued, cheeks tinted pink. "Now, I'm lucky if a guy won't take a winking face as a cue to send me a picture of his *you know*."

Faye nudged her shoulder. "Now *that* is romantic."

Ava pretended to puke. "I'm serious. This generation is so screwed." She lifted her cup of coffee, specks of brown tainting the hem of her gloves as she waved it around. "Here's to you, 2016's Romeo. Where for art my Facebook poke?"

"Nudeth for nudeth?"

As Faye cackled, Ava rolled her eyes, tripped her friend en route up the stairs.

"Hilarious."

Faye made herself at home as Ava rushed over to her computer. The number of times she'd hit refresh earlier that day wasn't one she was proud of.

But as she went to indulge herself in more clicking, she found that there was no need.

Her heart skipped to the sound of quick typing.

♤

(1) Friend Request

Ava Rios is now friends with Callum Gray.

Ava: Hey stranger.

Callum: Where's the lie?

Callum: I'm going to have to see the face of the criminal who's holding my book hostage.

Ava: Sweet with words, I see.

Ava: Okay, Casanova.

Callum: Okay.

Callum: Is this weird?

Ava: It doesn't have to be.

♤

The butterflies in Ava's stomach were on a rampage, and Callum was loading on her screen.

Seeing him on camera was different from the slivers she'd caught of him through peripheral glances and shy smiles on the plane. Different from the two profile photos he had up: one of him spraying graffiti on a dirty wall over the Seine, the other of him as a baby, painted over with a mustache and leather jacket.

This Callum was wearing a button-up shirt that didn't quite fit the black ink cityscapes tattooed down his arms, leaking into a swirl of unintelligible patterns down to his knuckles. His hair seemed to have been combed back just a minute before.

He'd been biting his lip before he realized that the camera had connected him to Ava.

"Hey."

Ava waved. "Hi."

On her end, she wore a blue party dress costumed in thick jewelry. The blanket she had with the Eiffel Tower threaded on it hung behind her.

"So it feels like we're in the same place," she joked.

Callum laughed.

"And," Ava continued, "I like to dress like a madwoman so that there's no confusion about what's underneath."

Callum nodded. "Madness?"

Ava smiled and echoed, "Madness."

"So I want to know your madness." He perched closer to the screen, licked his bottom lip. On impulse, she did the same.

"I'll send you a Powerpoint," she smirked, but there was a trip in her words. "It's nice to *officially* meet you. I'm Ava. And you are…"

"Really happy to see you."

♤

In the summer, they sat at their windows, listened to their cities play different songs. She'd convinced him to take paint to paper rather than spray to street, and then spent hours watching his canvases evolve from thick lines to entirely different worlds, portals past the gates of his mind.

She practiced ballet in front of him, and he pretended he knew a single thing about dance. Critiqued her technique, stroking the stubble on his chin until she'd fold into a fit of laughter.

In the fall, they talked endlessly with tired tongues. Two years older than her, Callum was working at some grocery store by day, dance club by night. It turned out that he'd been an heir to old money and a father with a bad temper. His family had lived all over the world, but no travel could change the swing of the man's fist.

His mother had run back to New York and left he and his sister with their father in Paris until he'd abandoned them too. One diagnosis later, Callum was still learning how to forgive her.

Ava had always lived in the city, always would. She seemed to attract people who did a lot of leaving – her father being the first. She carried her heart around in her hands, despite what could happen to it.

She, her mother, and her brother lived in a loft, and she had wide eyes for art and everything it promised. She spoke of NYU, and he'd spend hours with his bleary eyes on bits and pieces of her application as she dreamt of interweaving her love of dance with her love of story, turning old words into new routines.

"Like, hybrid art," Ava explained. "Is that stupid?"

It didn't matter what hour it was on her end or his, Callum's chest never stopped thrumming for the way her eyes lit up at the idea.

"It's brilliant."

In the winter, he bought her holly flowers and set them in front of the computer. She dressed in faux silk, and his fingers itched to touch her. He traced her dimpled smile through the screen.

Ava's eyes sparked with something he couldn't deal with from so far away.

"What do you want?" she asked, and she let the strap of her dress fall off one shoulder.

His fists curled at his sides.

In the spring, she wrote him a love letter that pretended not to be. He took it everywhere with him until Thomas and Brynn got a hold of it.

Then he hid it everywhere with him.

She tried on costumes for him, and he showed her his first finished painting. It was of his mother, what she'd looked like before she'd gotten sick. She wore a designer gown and puppet strings on her limbs. And still, she was running.

Ava cried.

He listened to French rap, and she tapped her feet to instrumental ballads. Both bled heartache to a different beat.

And always, it ended with weak voices and worn smiles.

"See you in a minute," she'd whisper.

"Yeah," he'd say, "See you in a minute."

♤

"She's just like," Callum sighed, raking his hands through his hair as if the movement would rid her of his constant thoughts. "Like seeing your favorite painting behind glass. It's touched you unlike anything else ever has, but you'll never be able to touch it back."

He stubbed his cigarette out against the stone wall that leaked into the Seine. A few teenagers laughed across the river. A flustered father caught his toddler from wandering too close.

"Fucking poetic, that is," Brynn said.

The two boys were opposite sides of the same dark coin. They'd both been born into excess – Brynn's mother and father were some sort of extended royal line in England, and Callum was an unwilling heir to blood money – and they'd both fled from it.

They had dropped out of the American University to stir up trouble in the city together, two boys itching for something more.

Of course, Brynn was boisterous and brilliant with his music, boom boxes down quiet romantic streets, leaving streaks of color wherever he went.

Callum was a brooder with a sharp tongue, preferred to leave his mark with dark paint on canvas and clung onto hope with the stories that existed *beneath* the streets.

Different brands of the same chaos.

"Fucking surreal," Callum said, lighting another. He pulled the beanie from the mess of blonde on his head again.

"Dude, what fucking plane ticket did you buy? Last flight I took was up to London, and the dude next to me was farting start to finish. Didn't even need gasoline, the engine. Could've shot us straight across the pond with that flatulence."

"Jesus, man."

Since Callum met Ava, Brynn had been off in London pursuing a potential record deal, recording samples and leaving Callum to fend for himself with Thomas.

Perhaps Ava had pulled the sentimentality out of him as well, but it now dawned on Callum how much he'd missed his friend.

"Just true." Brynn raised his brows. "So you love her, she's your dream girl. Tell her."

"She doesn't even know me," Callum said. "I don't know her. What am I supposed to say? The glow of the computer screen makes your eyes look beautiful? Oh yeah, and I've fallen in love with you."

"Oh," Brynn replied, mimicking a breathy female voice. "Callum, take me now. Take me *now*."

Callum slapped him across the back of his head. "Hope someone tosses you in the Seine. They don't, I will."

Brynn snorted, stole a smoke. "Wouldn't be the first time." He held up a finger. "Look mate, since you met this girl, you've been painting all the time, haven't been worrying as much about your mother, lookin' at the future like there's something there now. Can't even see your past on your face anymore. That's an *I love you* in so many words." Brynn jabbed at Callum's shoulder. "So what. The fuck. Are you waiting for?"

Legs dangling over the dirty waters below, Callum swore he saw a flash of Ava's smile in the sun across the Seine.

"Yeah," he said, "I don't know."

♤

"Okay," Ava called from where she was hanging over her bed, reading from one of those awful sleepover topic games. She wore wide-brimmed orange glasses and a long white gown, her hair a mess tumbling down to the ground.

Callum had his computer down on the kitchen counter, giving her the perfect view of his mayo-spreading technique.

She continued, "Describe your soulmate."

He smirked, "Look in the mirror."

Ava picked a stuffed animal up from near her bedpost and threw it at her webcam. "Take this seriously, Grump."

His hands halted for a second before continuing.

"I am."

♤

On Ava's eighteenth birthday, she went dancing.

She lost herself in red and blue lights, some black-walled club that didn't fit her pink dress and kitten heels in the slightest. She and Faye waltzed to reggae and skipped to dubstep.

Along for the ride, their friend Lucas watched from the sidelines, eyes on Ava. Always on Ava.

She smiled in tune, pretended that Callum's absence didn't weigh as heavy as a human being. That she didn't keep looking for a face in a crowd that wouldn't be there.

"So, Ava," Lucas asked when they went to get drinks, "I was wondering if maybe I could take you out to dinner. Y'know a birthday dinner or – "

"Oh, Lucas," Ava called back over the music,

tucking her hair behind her ear. "I'm actually not available."

Faye added, "She's in love with a computer."

Ava cut her a look. "Faye."

"Oh, come on. You spend more time on that thing than you do talking to anyone in real life. It's unbelievable."

"Why are you being mean about this?"

Faye sighed, "Because you're letting this guy toy with your emotions when he's halfway across the world and could be married with seven kids for all we know." She paused, retracting. "At least establish what the hell you're doing if you're going to waste so much time on him."

Ava swallowed.

Lucas stared at the space between them.

"So that's a…no to dinner?"

♤

"What are we doing?"

Callum paused his typing, glanced up at where Ava was leaning over her computer screen, eyes narrowed at him, a little tipsy.

He looked away again, amused. "Skyping."

"No," Ava cut in, "no sarcastic one-liners, no cryptic conversation, no more pouring my heart out and letting myself fall for a boy in a box when I don't even know if I mean that much to him."

She paused, scolded herself for the confession.

"Ava…" Callum let out a breath. "Ava, sit down."

Eyes shut, she sat.

"Look, Ava."

She opened one eye again, found him sitting in front of his screen with a lit candle and small cupcake, her name written with icing across it.

"Happy Birthday." He leaned over. "I feel *exactly* the same way." Ava touched the screen over the place where the candle was flickering, made a silent wish as he continued, "Sometimes I wonder if I imagined you. My girl, paper and bones." Callum smiled. "But I don't know if I'm capable of inventing something so perfect."

"Yeah?"

Callum blew out the candle, elbows on his desk. "Yeah."

"If I were there right now," Ava asked, hand still on the screen, "What would we be doing?"

Callum raised a brow. "We're really doing this?" He smiled. "Perv."

She threw a blanket at her camera. "I'm serious."

He hesitated only a moment before whispering, "Why don't we find out?"

♤

"So your girl is coming, eh?"

"Yeah, man," Callum smirked, though it collapsed into a goofy grin. "You'll get to meet her."

On the other end of the line, Brynn made a ruckus of something in the background before agreeing.

"Look man, I'm just saying that if you pull a quick one and make Thomas your best man, I'll kill ya, I will."

Callum chuckled, then paused.

"Hold on. I'm getting another call." He frowned. "That's weird. It's from New York."

♤

The red dress seemed silly now amidst the hustle and bustle of the airport. A black curl stuck to Ava's lip as she maneuvered the crowd, an uncomfortable mixture of too slow and much too fast. The natives were in skinny pants, women with hair piled up in sleek buns, men in crisp white t-shirts, aviator sunglasses buried in well-quaffed hair. And then there were the tourists, loud babbling only matched by the sound of their squeaky white tennis sneakers against the linoleum.

They all looked at her, the bright scarlet, the boisterous curls, like *who does she think she is, Audrey Hepburn?* And through it all, Ava rolled her little case down to the main exit, which she half understood from a blur of arrows and signs dripping with French accent marks. She bit down her flush and –

"Hey, girl. Follow me off the plane, did ya?"

Ava spun around. The Brit who'd been sitting near her on the flight making endless corny jokes and conversation – a quality source of entertainment, she wouldn't deny it – was standing before her now, and the gel in his hair had clearly withstood the plane ride in.

She rolled her eyes, steadied herself, then continued on her way – in the opposite direction.

"Oh, come on, mate. You're breaking my heart."

Ava let out a small laugh and waved her cell phone apologetically. "Sorry Casanova, I have to make a call. To my boyfriend."

The Brit clutched his heart, but nodded in defeat. He jotted his number down on the back of an extra customs form and gave her a toothy grin.

"In case he doesn't pick up."

Ava rolled her eyes and crumpled it in her fist.

Sitting down at one of the benches by the revolving doors, she tapped her fingers against her thigh as it rang, rang, rang.

"Ava." Callum said, sounding breathless and strained, and she pretended not to catch the nerves in his voice. "Ava, did you just land? I've been trying you for a while."

"I was on this magical, reception-less contraption called an airplane," Ava joked, hands drumming on her own stomach. Had the waist of this dress always been so *tight?* "Maybe you've heard of it." She paused. "It seems to me, Callum Gray, that you're not here."

Another pause. And then he sighed.

"That's because I'm not."

Ava pressed her fingertips to her forehead, her

mother and Faye's warnings sounding clearer to her than ever.

"Ava," her mother had said at the airport after a few long battles back at home, eyes so dark there could have been a death in the family. "I can't tell you what to do with your money. The money you worked *very* hard to save up with your afterschool job. Though, that's beside the point. I can't tell you who to waste time on and what to do with your life anymore. But think long and hard about the disappointment you'll feel if that boy lets you down. If that's worth whatever you think you're going to find there."

Ava had looked away then. Her mother seemed to be talking about someone else entirely.

Ava inhaled now, tried, "So what, you're stuck in traffic, or…?"

Callum cleared his throat once, then again. "Ava, I'm not in Paris."

Ava shoved down on the handle of her suitcase to sit on top of it, shoulders hunching in disbelief.

"What?"

"Please, listen. I had to…go. My – "

Click.

Heat spreading underneath her skin, the embarrassment was what propelled her to hang up the phone. As if by wishing it away, she could pretend that he wasn't the only reason she was there.

As if she wasn't the cliché girl in the beautiful red dress, crying in an airport for a boy who wasn't coming.

♤

On the other side of the Atlantic, Callum cursed, scrambled to dial her again, his black suit like false armor on his body. It went to voicemail, went to voicemail, went to voicemail, and he left shaken message after shaken message, one word tripping over the next in the rush to explain.

"Callum, son," the priest said, taking the phone from his shaking hands, "are you okay?"

Callum's gaze flickered up. "I'm…fine, Father. Just sorting a few things out."

The priest nodded, folded Callum's fingers back over the phone.

"We'll be starting the service in just a moment." The man paused, and Callum kept his stare neutral on his yellowed beard. "Your mother visited this church many times near the end, Callum. She'd have been pleased that you could finally see it for yourself."

Callum gave him a terse nod.

"She said she saw you in everything. The marble, the sermons, the little children laughing during Sunday School. You and your sister were truly the loves of her life."

Callum pressed the pad of his thumb to the corner of his eye. "Thanks."

"Yes, thank you, Father," another voice interjected. Celine Gray sidled up to her brother as gently as if she were the wind blowing in. She linked her arm with his and gave him a little squeeze. "We'll be seated in just a moment."

Every family had its vodka, every family had its chaser.

Between the Gray siblings, it was very clear which was which. Years spent dedicated to her English and French lessons had turned Celine into the perfect hybrid – a bright and blonde California girl with a French lilt to her words and a rough cut to her diamonds.

Growing up, Callum bore the brunt of their father's temper, and Celine was no stranger to it. But where life had left him callous, it had left her extra kind. And when she was eighteen and desperate to run off to San Francisco to design clothes and get a taste of the Pacific, he'd helped her.

He'd take care of their ghosts for them. He'd always been good at that.

"How are you, darling?"

Callum exhaled. "She's gone."

Celine nodded, bit her bottom lip.

"They said she went happily," she reasoned. "Peacefully."

Callum clenched his jaw. "None of this is how it's supposed to be."

"Hey," Celine said, trying to pat the tension out of his back. "Where's the rowdy, crazy little kid I used to know? How did that smile become a bruised fist?"

Callum cut a glance at her. "Someone punched it."

Someone loved it.

Celine winced at his words, clung onto his shoulder.

An heir and heiress to a throne of dirt, they filed into the church and said goodbye.

♤

(15) Missed Calls, (10) Voice Messages

Ava took another brash swig of her cocktail. Even the gothic lights of Notre Dame seemed to stare down in horror. She slipped her phone back into her purse.

"Gotta say," the Brit from the airport beamed, downing another shot like it was water, then leaning back to stare up at the dying sky. "Did not think I'd be getting the pleasure of your company on this trip when you stabbed my heart at de Gaulle."

Ava's smile barely appeared before fading again. "Trip?"

He leaned over, ate a handful of nuts from the table. "Yeah, yeah. Thought I'd be seeing an old friend. Plans changed."

Ava practically snorted. "Don't I know it."

"But you are a fine alt – "

The pain was what convinced her to shut him up, the liquor was what encouraged her to do it with a kiss. She leaned across the table, and it was ugly, pleasure-less. The moment their lips touched, she pulled away again, shot up from the table.

"Love, are you – "

On the taxi ride back to her hotel, the Eiffel Tower sparkled some tears for her. She opened her phone only to shoot off an email with no subject.

"You made me forget about endings. And then you showed me one."

♤

Callum: ava i'm back home now

Callum: you've blocked me on just about everything else

Callum: pls just listen

Brynn tossed another flower arrangement onto the living room table, then leaned over Callum by the computer.

"This her?" he asked, a consoling hand on his friend's shoulder. There were no jokes exchanged, no dark quips.

Callum nodded, opened the page to her profile picture, one of her eating a croissant at the Bastille Day festival in New York, no doubt once a tribute to him.

So taken with the expression on her face, he almost missed the paled, horrified one on Brynn's. Looking right at the strange girl who'd kissed him a few nights ago.

Almost.

♠

Back in New York, no one said I told you so. Not out loud, anyway.

In the years to come, Ava would remember that set of days as an endless cry, the sort of cry that took everything out of you and left you feeling like you'd never shed a tear again.

Faye and Lucas watched her with pity, brought offerings in tissue boxes and bakery cast-offs.

Her mother spoke to her like she would a lovelorn child, one who went looking for her father's footsteps in the eyes of other men.

Nothing seemed fair.

The third day back brought a knock on the door. Ava barely lifted her head from the company of soap operas and junk food, just listened to a few muffled voices and her mother's footsteps down the hall.

"Ava, you have a guest," her mother whispered, poking her head in.

"Is it death, finally coming to collect?"

Her mother rolled her eyes. "Ava, please."

Her sigh was immature and overly dramatic. She swung her legs off the bed, tied her hair up and straightened her appearance into some form of decency.

A blonde girl wearing diamonds and brown leather greeted her at their small kitchen table, smiling when her mother handed her a cup of warm tea.

Something familiar lived in the girl's features — the highlights in her blonde hair, the shape of her eyes. It was like seeing another painting by a favorite artist.

"Hi," the stranger said, her voice like paper curling at the edges with a French accent, "Ava?"

Ava frowned, suddenly feeling very aware of her disheveled state. "Yeah?"

"I'm Celine," she explained, "I'm Callum's younger sister."

Ava's mother glanced between the two, raising her brow at Ava, searching to find a signal for help. When Ava gave none, just stumbled back against the kitchen counter in slight shock, her mother made herself busy "dusting" the foyer bureau.

"Sorry to show up so unannounced," Celine said, gesturing at the seat opposite her, inviting Ava to sit. "Impulse runs in the family, as you may know."

They traded a nervous smile as Ava sat down.

"My brother will never forgive me for this," Celine murmured, staring down at her finger, habitually tracing the rim of her cup. "But I would have never forgiven myself if I hadn't. I understand that you believe he stood you up, Ava."

Ava stared down at the tabletop. "Because he did."

Celine cleared her throat. "Did Callum ever mention to you that our mother lived in New York?"

Ava's brow furrowed. "Yes, it's where he was going when we first met."

"Well, she did," Celine said gently. Her fingers, bone-thin and pale, shook against the tea cup in her hands. She reminded Ava of a porcelain doll – their whole family on a shelf marked fragile. Celine's eyes dimmed when she looked up again. "She passed away, Ava. I don't know what universe collided with ours to make sure that your paths would cross in such a horrible way. But when Cal found out that Mother was nearing the end, he got on the first red-eye. He's a mad man for his family, pretends not to be."

Ava had her face in her hands, whispering, *No.*

"And by the time he got here, she was gone," Celine finished in barely a whisper. "My brother is so many things. Reckless, infuriating, stubborn, *rude.*" She smiled, shook her head. "But he's loyal to the ones he loves. And missing the opportunity to meet you again, it wrecked him almost as badly as our mother's death. Forgive him, Ava. He spent those five days missing you and missing her. I could see it. Anyone could."

Ava caught a teardrop on her thumb. "God, that's already done. Is he still – "

"He's back in Paris," Celine said, sympathy joining her tone. "There was a very small service, and he decided to thrust himself back into work, take care of a few loose ends our mother had in France. You weren't returning his calls, so he didn't know whether to risk being *here* or *there* in case you showed up."

"I'm such a fool."

Celine smiled, shook her head. Her hand was cold and light when it fell over Ava's on the table.

"We're all fools for each other, Ava," Celine said. "What are you going to do about it?" She squeezed her hand again. "I've got to run. Have my own flight back to California. Don't tear yourself up too much over this. My brother cares for you immensely, even if his gears are a little broken." Celine paused. "And I see it in your eyes."

Ava shook her head, confused. "See what?"

"That you two will be under the same moon again."

Ava smiled, squeezed her hand back before walking her to the door.

"Celine?"

The blonde turned.

"How did you know where I lived?"

Celine smiled. "A postmarked envelope sticking out of my brother's journal. A letter you sent him, I suppose." She nodded at her once before disappearing around the corner. "Says he carries it with him wherever he goes."

♤

Callum picked up on the fourth ring.

Ava didn't wait for him to answer before saying, "Hi."

He let the silence eat at them for a minute before he replied, "Hey."

Ava paused, feeling like she'd just set her hand down on a burning stovetop.

"Callum, I – "

"So," he cut in, "You're okay."

Ava bit her lip. "I'm okay."

His laugh was sharp, a little mean. "Well, great."

"Callum, I know how you must feel…"

"No," he rasped, "I don't think you do." There was a shuffle and another pained sound before he asked, "Were you that heartbroken?"

Ava frowned. She was sitting on her fire escape, legs dangling two stories above the city. Above her, the sky was stretching into bed and fading black.

Down below, someone broke a glass bottle of soda. It sounded exactly like whatever was happening inside of her.

"What's your problem?"

He laughed again, bitter and sharp. "My problem is that of every trick of fate to ever fuck with me, this one has to be the best."

"What do you mean?"

"Fun fact, it was my best friend that you kissed, Ava."

The memory came to her like a ripped film reel: slanted and leaned over a table, Notre Dame casting a glow across her skin, a stranger with a thick accent, and feeling like her arms were flailing at the edge of the world.

Ava swallowed and wanted to deadpan, *You're kidding*, but it didn't seem appropriate. Instead, she stated the obvious. "The Brit."

"Is Brynn."

"Callum – "

"I don't blame you."

"You don't?"

"I would've done worse damage. You were hurt, I was hurt. My mother was dead."

His voice was dead, too. Her mind scrambled for anything that would resurrect it.

"I know. Your sister came to see me. Callum – "

"But maybe that's the point of this, that you and I don't know each other."

"What?"

"This thing between us…it doesn't make sense. Us toying with each other from across the world, making each other promises that we won't be able to keep. Doesn't make sense. I'm here, you're going to graduate in a few months, make it to NYU. There's no version of this story that ends with us together."

"How could you say that? Just a few weeks ago, we were falling for each other. We were talking about love and – "

"Of course we think we're in love with each other," Callum said, exasperated. "We're strangers. There is nothing more romantic than being a stranger to someone. They don't know you at three AM, they don't know how you got that scar. They just know that it's beautiful, but not what you had to do for it. It's knowing someone that fucks everything up."

Ava braced herself on an iron pole, shut her eyes. "That's how you feel?"

His silence was an answer enough.

"Then I agree. You and I don't know each other at all," she said. "Bye, Callum."

Guilt crept up into Callum's throat.

"See you in a minute." It was an impulse, a chipped nail, a bad habit.

"Bye," she said again.

♤

That night, Paris crawled over to the coastline, fingernails in dirt, and cried out to New York, "I'm so sorry about the things I've done for love."

interlude.

"Today is terrible, and Pluto is still suffering."

Faye rolled her head back, let out a torturous sigh. "I can't wait until you drop that phrase."

"Faye," Ava deadpanned, waving her pencil like a stubby wand before landing it on her friend's nose, "I too am a desolate dwarf planet who was dumped by the solar system."

Faye ordered them three cups of coffee at their favorite place on Third, all wood and steam, vines creeping up the walls and dangling plastic coffee beans. Lucas trailed them, shaking a few packets of sugar like maracas in his palms.

Ava continued, "I too am an abandoned shell of light, destined to – "

"Oh, Jesus."

"This has nothing to do with religion."

Faye was still massaging her temples when they grabbed their cups and filed to the garden out back, walled in by four other brown buildings, casting odd shapes of shadow and light in the makeshift yard. Places like these in New York, the ones that tried to be suburbs, were Ava's favorite. Like dandelions dug from grit and picket fences carved from bone. She dropped down onto a wicker chair, threw her legs over Lucas's lap, and toyed with Faye's hair.

"I too – "

Faye threw a coffee stirrer at her.

Ava smirked, patting down the pleats of her scarlet sundress, then pulling the loose curls away from the back of her neck.

"Whatever, Neptune."

Her laughter was cut short only by Lucas's hand, which cupped her calf as he casually sipped his coffee. Ava shifted uncomfortably, exchanged a glance with Faye.

An entire two years after graduation had done nothing to mar their trio. In fact, they clung and orbited each other more often than ever to survive being thrust into the familiar strange of city colleges and commuter campuses. Faye was a psych major at Barnard, Lucas was undecided at Fordham, and Ava was drowning in the arts – pirouettes danced to the gothics.

But Ivy Joe's was the one corner of the city, tucked behind SoHo, that time couldn't touch.

"Tonight?" Faye mentioned, raising her cup in a false toast. "Are we suffering through Lucas's flannel friends or crashing at my dorm with cold pizza?"

"Your support overwhelms me," Lucas mumbled, squeezing Ava's leg as he adjusted in the chair. He picked up a fallen plastic flower and offered it to her.

Ava smiled, skipped over his gaze.

Faye held a finger up. "Honesty is my only policy Luke-Ass. We love you, but another hour dissecting the origins of craft beer might kill us." Before Lucas had a chance to retort, Faye cut him off with another raised finger and turned to Ava. "You told me to remind you to pick up that edition of *Lolita* for class."

Ava perked up and slid her legs from Lucas's lap to plant a kiss on Faye's cheek. "Life-saver."

Lucas's shoulders dropped, dejected. "Want me to come with?"

Ava shook her head, handed over the cup. "Guard my coffee? It's just down the block." She nudged his shoulder. "Besides, I don't want to interrupt the banter, Abbott and Costello."

With a flounce of her skirt, she was gone, and Faye shot Lucas a sympathetic smile.

She reached over and clinked her cup with his. "Cheer up, lover boy. Your tongue is showing."

Down the block, Ava had her beaten pleather jacket tied like a belt around her waist. The weather was unusually nice for February, a written invitation for Lower Manhattan to haul out the bikini tops, snapbacks, and beer crates. A toddler licked gelato from his fingers, a lost boy played the drums with a can of Campbell's on his stoop. Ava gave him a dollar and a smile before stepping into a corner bookshop.

The place was cold and smelled like freshly printed paper, a combination that made her shiver. She shrugged her jacket on like a shawl over her shoulders and trailed her finger along the hardcovers in Horror.

Bookstores were just shelved cemeteries of bound ghosts. There was not a place in the world she felt more at home.

Her finger was halted by a strange thought, one she hadn't had in months. *Perhaps there was one place in the world.*

"Nabokov, Nabokov, Nabokov," Ava sang under her breath as she stumbled through the aisles. The place was nothing more than a shadow, a dimly lit labyrinth built for customers to discover rather than find.

Frustrated and still mumbling, Ava rounded a corner towards the back, reading the synopsis of a contemporary while still half-scanning the shelves for her pick.

"Excuse me."

(Somewhere, over another ocean: This is your captain speaking. Prepare for landing. Brace for impact.)

Ava glanced up momentarily, shifting over so that the stranger could get by, then glanced again.

Her heart stuttered to a near stop.

"You."

Callum blinked back at her, hand hovering over her left arm. He parted his lips and made a choked sound, like the letters of her name had forgotten their purpose at the back of his throat.

She inhaled. "Callum."

He let his hand brush her side before it dropped. "Ava."

"You're in New York," Ava stated dumbly.

"Apparently," he rasped, eyes raking over every spot on her face.

Long distance, Callum had been a lightening bolt on the other side of a sea, passing thunder waiting for day to come. In person, he was a storm. Under the dimness of the shop, his eyes darkened indigo. He stood a good foot taller than her, and his hair was buzzed closed to the sides of his head, blonde waves swept back in a style he'd once been too boyish for. He smelled like wood chips and light cologne. Like a renovation, like a new home.

Ava's heartbeat picked up, reminded her it was still there.

"Hi," she said suddenly, the sharp, unnatural sound startling them both, and reached up to pull him into a hug. Callum's hand twitched midair before finding the center of her back, the mess of her curls. She shut her eyes against his unbuttoned dress shirt, and he held her there for a moment, thumb catching on the bridge of her ear.

"Hey," he whispered against it.

They hadn't realized how long they had been standing there until the bookseller shot them a pointed look over his glasses, clearing his throat as he passed by.

They extricated themselves from each other, and Callum lamely picked up a random book for show.

Karma Sutra for Beginners.

He tossed it aside, scratched the back of his neck with a shy, anxious grin on his face. "Fuck."

Ava pursed her lips, glanced down at the book. "Well, that'll show you how."

Their laughter rumbled the shop. Ava curled into herself, hair brushing his chest as she bent and clutched at her belly. Callum braced himself on a shelf for support, throat hoarse from chuckling so hard. It was a dam bursting, a radio blaring, a beautiful song. A finally, finally, *finally*.

And when there was nothing else left, they stood there, still leaned towards each other, trying to catch their breaths.

Ava straightened first, very aware that he was only a breath away. "It's really good to see you."

Callum cleared his throat, and she watched the jut of his jaw, the dark circles under his eyes, a cut near the stubble on his chin.

He said, "It's really good to be where you are."

Ava nodded. A leather spine pressed into her bent one.

♤

"I was going to look you up before I got here. Maybe send you a message," Callum admitted as they fell into step on the concrete. Under the sun, he peeled his dress shirt off to reveal the t-shirt beneath, anything to keep him busy enough to not look at her too long.

Last time they'd been standing this close, it had been on a plane, and he hadn't known how much it would hurt him later.

Ava glanced at him. "Yeah?"

He nodded, jaw clenching. "I decided not to."

When he chanced a look at her, he instantly regretted it. She was a blur of color: browns and reds and olives. His gaze caught on every inch of her habits, collecting them to make up for two years lost. She tucked her hair behind her ear, bounced off her right foot with every step, hummed under her breath when she was nervous.

Ava was humming now.

"Not that…I didn't want to see you," Callum corrected, angling himself towards her as they stepped into some earthy coffee shop spilling faded jean hipsters and a trellis of potted plants. He eyed the place cautiously while Ava waltzed in as if she were coming home. "After everything that happened…"

Ava nodded. "I get it." She looked like she wanted to say more, but she was cut off by a terse voice, a girl and boy making a bee-line for them from some outdoor space in the back.

"Next time you want to give me cardiac arrest, do it locally," the girl scolded, not even noticing

Callum as she curled around Ava like a mother hen. The boy, however, couldn't take his eyes off Callum. There was a slant in his glare and square in his shoulders that seemed a little too much like a threat.

Callum narrowed his eyes at both of them.

Ava smiled half-heartedly. "Sorry, Mom." She glanced at him over her shoulder, and his lips tugged at their corners. "Callum, these are my best friends, Faye and Lucas. Guys, this is…" She inhaled. "Callum."

Faye froze. Looked at Callum, then at Ava, then back at Callum. "I'm sorry, did I miss this on the calendar?"

"Must have," Lucas echoed, eyeing Callum in disbelief.

Faye cleared her throat again and outstretched her hand, still not smiling. "So, you're Paris."

"Yeah, it's on the birth certificate and everything," Callum remarked under a sharp chuckle, reaching out to shake it. "Nice to…finally meet you, too."

Ava ducked her head and laughed through her nose. A child tipped a cup of water over across the room, a fly made its first spring appearance by the light bulb. Callum clenched and unclenched his fist.

And then he set his hand on her back.

"Do you want to take a walk?"

"Yeah," Ava replied. "Yes. Sure." She turned to Faye, setting her hands on either one of the girl's shoulders, who was still throwing reluctant looks at Callum. She promised, "I am just a text message away."

"Or a milk carton," Faye sighed, pulling her in for a hug. "Send me messages on the hour. And quit seeing the world so pink." The last statement was pointed at Callum, who stuck his hands in his front pockets, pretended not to hear. "Because it isn't."

Lucas, who'd been oddly quiet behind them, seemed to have found a switch that brought him back to life, a wired smile on his face.

"You're missing out on guitar strumming and kale," Lucas joked, holding onto Ava's arm a second too long to escape Callum's notice.

"Somehow I'll manage," Ava whispered back, touching her nose to his.

Callum's cupped his own jaw, looked away.

Ava bit her lip. "Ready?"

"For a while now."

♤

The weather cooperated, but New York was on fire because of it, people spilling out onto the streets in masses. They'd made it up to Washington Square Park and trailed a quiet path through the East Village, littering the city with their conversation.

"This is *supposed* to be the part in which some sidewalk singer starts playing a love song," Ava joked as some guy popped a wheelie, then threw up all over his skateboard, much to the enjoyment of his friends. "But it's New York, so I'll take what I can get."

"I don't know," Callum said, thrumming his fingers along to the sounds of the guy retching. "I could slow dance to this any day."

Ava shoved his shoulder.

They stopped at a bar next to a Blues club, and he ordered them a round of beers and dollar slices of pizza.

There was a pause.

"Callum, what are you doing here?"

He swallowed down a gulp of beer. "Archiving the things in my mother's townhouse. Celine and I are renting it out for some extra money, and she couldn't make it up here for the packing." He flicked the rim of the bottle, and it made a little tune. "And I, um, I'm showing at a gallery here."

Ava dropped the slice in her hand onto her plate. "*Hey*, hot-shot."

Callum smirked. "Alright, alright. It's just this hole in the wall on the Lower East. Nothing big. A buddy of mine just opened his place up to the public and thought if I was going to be here already…" He ducked his head like a shy kid presenting in class for the first time. "I had every reason to be here." A pause. "I was running out of reasons not to be."

Ava smiled from behind the rim of her bottle. "How long?"

Callum straightened. "A week. Headed home on Friday."

The smile faltered.

When it returned, it was plastered and strained.

"God, are you really the same grumpy old man who used to call me on Skype, splattered in paint and bruises?" She rolled her eyes, remembering that wild, dark look in his eyes when Paris had been his canvas, and he'd refuse to call his dreams by their names.

She added, with a hand over his knuckles, "I'm so proud of you."

Callum nodded slowly, turned his palm up towards hers.

"Always have been."

Ava echoed, "Always have been."

♤

If there was any ice to break, the job had been done. They ordered drinks and leaned into each other like, yet again, there's was a game of cards, trading words and old stories, trying to come up with some version of reality in which whatever had happened between them could coexist with the truth.

Ava told him about her sleepless nights, about her double major, and when her eyes lit up describing the way she'd done a ballet installation to Edgar Allen Poe's *The Raven*, all feathers and rustled pages, spinning in the dark, Callum had to brace himself against the bar.

She was the only goddamn person in the world who could take him flying without feet.

"You thought I was weird," Ava suddenly accused him, and Callum realized that he'd lost track of the conversation in his little reverie.

"I did," Callum admitted with a laugh. He touched a curl where it hit her collarbone. "But I liked your weird. You were like a little spitfire. Still are."

"And you were stone," she remarked.

"Still am."

Ava narrowed her eyes, studied him for a moment as if she were a doctor, looking over healing wounds. His edges were still sharp, she still handled him like a child would a drawer of knives, scared to cut her fingers on him. But he was softer in the eyes, his smile came easier. She wondered how many strokes it had taken to paint over his demons.

"No," Ava replied simply, smiling at the bartender for another round.

The guy nodded and made eyes at her, and Callum cut him a look, wrapped an arm around her waist.

Pinned to the wall, beside an ad for a strip club and a poster for The Kooks, was a postcard from Rome. A modern woman waved from the top of an old empire.

It read, "What relief can come from ruin."

♤

"Okay, we're going to go see a play. Something dark and Shakespearean," Ava slurred, clinging onto Callum's arm as they stumbled through the streets. He laughed openly as she performed to a lamp post, murmuring something about Hamlet's bones and Juliet's blood. He steered her away from it with an arm slung around her shoulders.

They'd had about the same amount to drink, but he was nowhere near as far gone as she was. Still, a buzz crept up his skin, light bursting from the cracks of him.

"Where are we going to go see this play?"

Ava frowned. "It's New York City. We'll go to Times Square."

"It's three AM."

She sidled up to him at a corner where the broken street light was flickering *stop, go, stop, go.*

"Well look at that," Ava replied, hands on his chest, then his shoulders. "I finally know you at three AM."

There it was.

The night had been a skilled game of Chicken — how close each of them could broach the subject of what happened two years ago. Thus far, there hadn't been any spilled venom. But now, she was folding up his cruel words into a paper crane and handing them right back to him.

"We have to do everything right now," she said tiredly, attempting to focus on the moment. "Because something bad is going to happen again."

Callum was breathing heavy, and Ava seemed to sober up a bit at the admission. His hand slid up to her arm, to hold her hand over where it was set on his shoulder.

Finally, he asked, "Where's home?"

One heel skidding against the concrete, Ava's smile didn't quite reach her eyes.

Not when she took his hand.

Not when she pointed to the center of his chest.

♤

The next morning, she opened her eyes to stark white.

Ava groaned, hid her face under a blur of sheets and mussed up hair. She was still wearing her clothes from the day before, her legs were tangled up in a foreign comforter, and a gray sweater that didn't belong to her was now wrapped around her shoulders.

The place echoed her footsteps like a museum gallery would. And truthfully, it was worthy of the title. The walls stretched and stood adorned by gilded marble and polished wood. The room she was in was painted a shade of ivory, golden lilies carved into the finishes. Even the nightstand beside her was luxurious, gold-plated and rounded in shape. Her cell phone and purse seemed to litter it. *Unworthy.*

Ava collected her stash and slipped through the door, spilling out into a hallway where the furniture that lined the walls was covered in white sheets, some piled near the grand staircase. She felt small, like another old ghost.

Downstairs, she found Callum staring up at a slanted chandelier in the grand living room, taking steps backwards and forwards underneath it. His clothes were dark, as were his eyes. Ava watched him for a moment before clearing her throat.

"Hi."

Callum halted his steps and turned to her, embarrassed. "Hey." He stepped backwards and reached for a coffee cup and box of scones on top of a taped packing box. "Hope you don't mind that I stuck you in my sister's old room. You insisted on not telling me where your dorm room was."

Ava flushed and shrugged one shoulder. "Peace offering?"

Callum smiled. "Sure."

She sat on the bottom step of the grand stairwell, and he crawled over to join her, his back against her leg. They sipped coffee and nibbled scones in silence for a moment, and she eyed the way the dim light filtering in through the drawn curtains was sparking the scar by his jaw like a white lightening bolt.

"What were you doing under the chandelier?"

Callum turned to her. "Our home in France had one just like this. Creepy almost, how much of a replica this place is. My mother would wake me up at three AM and dress me up in a full suit and tie." He shook his head. "I was six. And she'd make me waltz with her underneath it for hours. I thought it was hilarious."

He downed another gulp of coffee.

"And then one day, my father pressed this switch in her. Just knocked the light from her eyes. And she stopped waking me up to dance underneath it. She'd do it herself for hours and hours until her feet were bleeding, and that's how I'd find her in the morning for breakfast. And I knew then that nothing about life was very funny at all."

"Callum – "

"I'm good," he said, busying himself with crumpling the box and grabbing her now-empty cup. "Are you still hungry? There's not much here, but – "

"Callum."

"And if you need clothes or anything…"

"Callum, I'm sorry," Ava said under a ragged breath. Tears spilled of their own accord as she stepped down from the staircase, faced his curved back, tense in the shoulders. "I should have been there. I should have given this the chance that it deserved. I shouldn't have gone kissing…"

Callum drew in a breath.

"I should have brought flowers to your mother's funeral," Ava said. "I should have been there to hold your hand. I should have come back."

"I'm the one who had to live with letting you go," Callum replied. "I'm the one who had to lie and say that you and I were strangers when no one in the world knows me better. You think that hasn't eaten at me for two years?" He turned around to look at her. "You think someone can go back to loving other people after that?"

Ava shook her head. "No."

"No," Callum echoed. "It should have been us at the Louvre, getting lost in the eras."

She took a step towards him. "It should have been us on the Seine, dancing at midnight."

"It should have happened like this," Callum said, bringing a calloused palm to her cheek, then sliding a few rough fingers into her hair.

Ava exhaled, and they shared the same breath. "Like what?"

And then he kissed her slow.

Two years worth.

♤

"You're not really here," Ava whispered a few hours later, lips fallen open against his shoulder. He reached back to skim his knuckle against her cheekbone, up the bridge of her nose, then to smooth out the crease in her forehead.

"No?" he asked. "Do I feel like a phantom?"

She smiled. "Sometimes." She traced the raised skin by his spine, a blistered scar, then the bone of his collar. "You feel like a painting."

Callum turned around to kiss the hollow of her throat. "You feel like a canvas." He held her hand, then pressed it back against the hardwood.

Her eyes fluttered shut when he settled between her legs, and she whispered, "And how do you feel *about* me?"

He pinned her other hand up when her teeth found skin.

"Under the definition of love, you'll always be my 'see also.'"

♤

She wore a black gown to the gallery opening, despite Callum's insistence that the place did not call for it. It was on the side street of a side street, had a rickety chalkboard sign out front, and its guests were in denim jackets, sipping wine from plastic cups.

Ava looked more like one of the installations.

Callum kept his hand on her lower back and introduced her as his – no title, no hesitation. Just his.

And then he showed her to a cluster of paintings on a far wall, bristles and strokes she recognized from hours spent memorizing his hands and brushes moving like a dance in the dark through a computer screen.

Callum had transformed famous cities, rebuilt them in scenes filled with marble and rain. There was a dark cloud inside of his version of Versailles, and it rained on the heads of ghost kings and queens. New York City was a hurricane of sea-soaked streets and tenants swinging their legs over windowsills.

Enraptured, Ava's finger reached up to nearly touch one until Callum stole it away.

"Self Portrait" made her cry, for it was a picture of him but not – his face cracked open like a broken globe spilling diamonds and porcelain tea cups and gasoline instead of blood. Scars at the price of riches, and how it had torn him apart.

"You're brilliant," she told him.

Callum gave no response, just took her arms and turned her to a piece she hadn't yet noticed.

The description card simply read, "Ava."

On some night she must have fallen asleep in front of her computer screen, Callum had sketched her as she was, then painted over it with world maps and state lines and miles and miles apart.

There, Point Zero gilded gold on the nape of her neck. There, the Empire State Building standing tall along her spine. The stars over their sea freckled her nose and cheeks. The Atlantic washed over the tendrils of her hair.

Their distance, their story.

As Callum turned to talk to a buyer, another joined the space beside Ava.

"Beautiful work," she said without catching Ava's face.

"Yeah," Ava whispered.

"It's almost like he painted her real enough so that she could step off the canvas. Be with him."

Ava nodded, glanced back at Callum. "Almost."

♠

At the airport, Callum couldn't look at her.

"You're breaking my heart," he rasped, tapping his boarding ticket against his thigh. They'd spent every second of the past week together. His mind had known her by heart for a long time, but now his hands did, too. Bookstore visits, outdoor picnics, packing boxes, tangled in sheets and with their words, and more things that were too much and not nearly enough to make up for the time they'd lost.

Ava wiped another tear from her cheek. "Well, just to settle the score."

"This isn't where we're going to end, Ava," Callum promised her, "everything starts now."

Ava smiled, still crying. "Is that what you're going to write in my yearbook?"

He cracked a smile, tickled her side. "I'm the romantic, and you're the wise guy, huh? How the times have changed."

She pressed her forehead to his. "How they have."

"I'll, uh," Callum breathed against her lips, cupping the back of her neck with his eyes clenched shut. "I'll see you in a minute."

Ava nodded. "Yeah, I'll be right there."

Callum hid his face from her, just kissed her once and hiked his duffel bag onto one shoulder, gripping her arm before finally letting go.

"Wait," Ava called, reaching into her purse and surfacing with a journal, his journal, still untouched from when he'd first dropped it. "I can finally give it to you in person."

Callum smiled, walking backwards, raising his clocked wrist. "That's my flight. Guess I'll just have to see you again."

Ava smiled back, clutched it to her chest as he disappeared into the airport crowd.

A phantom indeed.

deux.

(10) Missed Calls, (5) Voice Messages

(15) Missed Video Calls

ava.rios@xmail.com: Hey handsome! I'm over here making magic with my feet onstage and miss you dearly. Give me a call when –

grayxcallum@zmail.fr: Hey baby. Happy graduation. For the hundredth time, apologizing for not being able to score those tickets. I wish I had the cash. Let me know if you still want to web –

(6) Missed Calls, (2) Voice Messages

(10) Missed Video Calls

ava.rios@xmail.com: Hey you. Great news about the company. They're thinking about picking up some of the work I did in college. The Poe piece. Can you –

grayxcallum@zmail.fr: Seeing you for Christmas was amazing. Thanks for making it here. I'm sorry that I couldn't give you a big family to spend it with. Was everything okay –

(3) Missed Calls, (1) Voice Message

(1) Missed Video Call

ava.rios@xmail.com: Are you around?

grayxcallum@zmail.fr: Call me back.

No Missed Calls

♤

Callum drummed his fingers against his desktop in a dizzying beat as he waited for Ava to call in. Around him, the apartment he'd once shared with Thomas and Brynn beckoned for a new presence – the walls were bare save for a few of his more personal art pieces, a set of film tickets, and a stack of books lining the floor.

`   He clenched his jaw.

Time told the story better than he ever could.

"Hello?" Ava's face materialized onscreen, and he tried to smile. Five years had not touched an inch of her. Her hair was longer, down to her waist, and she wore red lipstick. But her eyes were still young, the song that came from her every word was still singing. He traced the shape of her chin on the screen.

"Hey."

She smiled. "You look good."

Five years had left them closer, then farther apart.

She was working at a dance company that had taken to her multimedia performances. And he had made the slightest of dents in the art scene with his pieces, sold everywhere from street corners to the walls of tattoo shops, while he helped run a restaurant movie theatre in the next district.

Distance found no place for itself in their endeavors, and they'd grown to exist only in missed calls, reaching for phones in the dark, short visits with expiration dates always looming, empty promises, and disappointment.

Callum forced another smile. "You look better."

Ava leaned over and yawned. "I have to run in a few minutes."

He swallowed the sting. "Yeah? Can't stand my face?"

She laughed. "You got me. There's just this cast party for our upcoming production. Lucas – "

"There's a surprise."

"I don't know what your problem is with him. He's played a huge role in my success. That should make you happy. Proud."

"Hey, I've *always* been proud of you. But the stunning coincidence of What's His Face managing a performing arts company that just so happened to pick up your show doesn't escape me."

Ava recoiled. "So this has nothing to do with my talent, right? I got nowhere without Lucas's high school crush on me?"

Callum sighed. "That's not what I'm saying."

"He's my friend," Ava snapped. "Who is *here*, supporting me. Here."

"Say it one more time," Callum retorted. "Didn't hear you."

"Mature."

"Look, I'm sorry that I can't magically become an overnight sensation and make enough cash to fly in and out like you do. I'm sorry that my art – "

"This has nothing to do with your art. If you had used the money from your inheritance – "

"I want nothing to do with that money, and you know that, Ava. Not until I can make something out of what I have already. You used to believe in that."

"Until you chose proving a point over being with me."

There was a long pause. She turned away from the screen, he put his face in his hands.

"What are you holding onto over there, Callum?" Ava finally asked, facing the wall. "Because it isn't me."

"Don't do that," Callum said. "Don't act like I'm not trying to make this work just as hard as you are. Don't act like I wouldn't trade the world to be with you. Don't act like I haven't lost nights reading every single version of our story, hoping one of them ends with you and I."

"Then what," Ava asked, "are you waiting for?"

"Oh, so I'll come to New York?"

"Why not?"

"Because there is no room for me in your life, Ava," Callum spat. "Because you are moving up, and I am stagnant, and we both know how quickly this is going to fall apart if I move over there with a few paintings and not a dollar to my name. *My* name. Not my parents'. I am fucking walking on eggshells trying to keep you in my life – anyway I can."

"So don't," Ava said, voice breaking. "Don't anymore."

Callum glanced up at her. She was still looking at the wall.

"What?"

"We're ruining each other," Ava said simply, quietly. "And I would rather let you go than be the one to ruin you."

"Ava – "

"Stop reading," she said, her voice breaking into a sob. "There *is* no version that ends with you and I." On her end, the screen went black. "Callum?"

"Must be the shitty service," Callum said. The "disable camera" window glared back at him on his screen.

Ava drew in a breath, and he could still see her, hands on the computer, like she was trying to reach inside.

"I didn't mean that," she admitted.

"You have to go, right?"

"Callum – "

"So do I."

Ava's head dropped. "See you in a minute, right?"

Callum hesitated.

And then he ended the call.

On the next day, her birthday, Callum raised a solitary candle dug into a cupcake to his lips and blew it out.

The computer screen was still dark.

♤

Dating Lucas was like trying to sprout roses with dandelion seeds. The growth was there, but nothing would be blossoming red.

Ava said yes to him in the summer after she and Callum stopped pretending they weren't giving up on each other. They rode bikes and laughed over things that friends did and moved into a flat that was all sunshine and wood.

Lucas always called her by her first name, and her spine always rejected his touch, still hung up on Callum's fingerprints.

Her mother loved him, he was always home for dinner.

Her heart called her on the phone sometimes, from someplace else.

♤

When the girl who worked cashier in their theater looked at him a little too long to be friendly,

Callum swallowed down Ava's name and decided to ask her out.

Marie was from the French countryside and spoke slanted English and always kept her lips stained red.

When Callum kissed her, it was like listening to Bach when he'd asked for Beethoven.

A masterpiece, just not his.

His lips knew the drill, but his heart panged in protest. Angry, it stamped a postcard to Ava.

"Wish you were here."

♤

Ava: What's she like?
Callum: I'm not talking about this with you.
Ava: Why? We're friends, right? Is there a problem?
Callum: Smart.
Ava: Great.
Callum: Pretty.
Ava: Expected.
Callum: Fun. Outgoing. French. What the fuck do you want me to say, Ava? That she's not you? That I'd rather be with you? That you haunt me through everything else I decide to love? What can I say that you don't already know?

Ava: Callum…
Callum: Why, what's he like?
Callum: What's he like, Ava?

♤

The moon over the fourteenth arrondisement held a peculiar sort of magic – sprinkled like dust across pastel rooftops and pink lights. And from the nightstand by his balconied window, Callum's cellphone howled at it.

He startled out of a dark, dreamless slumber and groaned as the thing blared and chimed. Groggy and blurry-eyed, he caught only the telltale jut of the letters in Ava's name – and the photo of her coy smile, the pattern of freckles on her face, her amber eyes.

Callum sat up, thumb hovering over the button for a moment before answering.

"Hey you."

There was a long, raspy intake of breath on the other side, and Callum pulled the phone away from his ear for a second to double check that the source of the call hadn't just been wishful thinking.

Still Ava.

"So you're the one."

It was a man's voice that greeted him, dark and irritated, a familiar sort of resentment that he couldn't quite place.

"You're going to ruin her life, you understand? Everywhere she goes, you're with her. Everywhere she goes, she runs into you."

"Who the hell is this?"

"This is Lucas."

Callum swiped a palm over his face. "Jesus, man. Ava and I are friends. Friends who live thousands of miles apart. Can't get anymore platonic than the fucking Atlantic Ocean." He glanced at his alarm clock. "Do you know what time it is here? Or what her bill is going to look like when – "

Lucas cut him off. "I'm not an idiot. How does that lie taste?"

It tasted horrible.

"Look," Lucas continued. "If you loved her the way I do, you'd let her go. It isn't romantic. You're always just going to feel like something she failed. Have some decency, give her closure."

Callum bit his tongue, pulling the phone away from his ear. *I don't love her the way you do. I love her something terrible.*

"If you were that worried about this, you'd be talking to your girlfriend," Callum finally said. "Not me."

"Fiancé," Lucas corrected after a long beat. "Think about what I said."

Click.

Callum sent his phone flying across the room, and it brightened before buzzing dead.

The next morning, when he met up for coffee with Marie and told her how he still felt about Ava, she thanked him.

"Now I finally know the name of the girl who lives in your eyes."

♤

"You're really doing this now, Faye?"

Ava glared up at her best friend as she clasped a set of dangling black jewels to her ears, a sharp contrast against her pale white gown. It was barely a dress, barely a sheet. It fit like a ghost clinging to her curves.

Faye tied a puff of her curls on top of her head. "I'm just having a conversation with you. Look, I've always loved Lucas in the way you love that one sweet cousin during the holidays. We've always been a triad, but *you and I* were friends. He was just in love with you. Unrequited love."

"Faye, stop it."

"But now, in a rush to get over Paris – "

"Callum."

"You're accepting a proposal that you know in your heart you don't want to accept. I mean, just look at the piece you're about to perform. Where is your head?" Faye paused. "Where is your heart?"

"So what? You want me to go to France? Break him up with his girlfriend? Be with him?"

"I want you to choose what's right for you."

"Yeah," Ava scoffed, "so long as it's what you think is right for me."

Exasperated, Faye caught sight of the leather book Ava was using to balance her makeup tubes. She let out a small noise of disbelief.

"You've been chasing that book for ten years, Ava. And what the has it gotten you?"

"Love," she said, an impulse, a mistake. She winced against the confession, then corrected, "with Lucas. Who is *right* for me. Now I have to go on and perform this piece. I'd really love it if you could at least support me in that."

As Ava stepped out and through a stage door, Faye paused to find her phone before she followed. In the dark of the audience, she hesitated before pulling the device out and lowering the brightness on the screen, thumbs shaking as they searched for a name in the contact list.

She video dialed Callum, who picked up on the first ring. No hesitation.

Another noise of disbelief.

He squinted at the phone in the dark of his apartment, whispered, "Faye? Is that – "

"Just shut up," Faye whispered back, raising the phone as high as she could without giving herself away to the neighboring seats. She turned the camera towards the stage.

The curtains opened, the music played. And then Ava began to dance.

The set was an elaborate hybrid, a metallic reimagining of Paris meeting New York. Garden apartments, open balconies, and flower shops leaked into concrete, skyscrapers and whirring trains from the Seine into the Hudson. And behind it all, the Eiffel Tower leaned towards the Empire State Building, iron hands reaching out to each other from the structures. Just barely touching.

When the music paused for a moment, Faye heard Callum let out a noise.

Aptly titled "A Dance of Two Cities," Ava painted the distance with every thrust and turn of her body, beginning through careful steps, spinning back and forth, then meeting herself in the middle for a sensuous drop to the floor, a pull from the heavens on her torso.

And then it transitioned into something hectic, broken steps, hands in her hair, an invisible storm pulling her this way and back. The crowd held a collective breath when she flipped backwards over an iron spire and finished in Paris.

She always finished in Paris.

Wracked with a sob, Ava bent over herself when she finished the piece, tears in her eyes as she waved to the crowd, all on their feet.

Faye showed Callum.

"Now you know," she whispered, barely catching him thank her before she shut off the phone.

♤

"Mr. Gray?"

Callum held the phone against his ear with his

shoulder. "Call me Callum, Mr. Brooks. So great to finally talk to you."

Behind him, Brynn barreled through the door and dropped a newspaper onto the stack of mail in Callum's hands.

He gave his old friend the finger.

"Callum, I wanted to reach out to you personally. Your pieces speak to me on a level that other budding young artists have yet to reach. You paint with such story, with such lore. You're an asset to the art world. It was an honor to even receive your pieces for submission."

Callum raised a finger to his lips at Brynn, heartbeat racing. "That's a really big compliment, Mr. Brooks. Thank you."

"All that is to say that I am extremely happy to invite you to our artists' residency program in Brooklyn. We'd love to highlight your work in an exhibit entitled 'Ava,' revolving around the title piece."

"Are you kidding? Sir, I – "

Sorting through the mail in his hands, Callum broke off when he came across a package. Inside were a leather journal and a thick ivory envelope, postmarked from familiar names and a foreign address.

Lucas O'Reilly and Ava Rios.

You are cordially invited to join –

"Mr. Gray?"

Ava Rios in celebrating her matrimony to –

"Are you still there?"

Callum slid the invitation over to Brynn, who mouthed expletive after expletive upon further inspection.

"I'm here, Mr. Brooks," Callum finally said. "Sorry about that. "I, um, I'm very interested. But I'd like to take some time to think about the logistics of it all. Maybe we can set up a meeting?"

Callum stared down at the cardstock and ribbon. At this point, he didn't know if fate preferred them together or apart.

"I'll be in town for a wedding."

trois.

Ava always thought she might get married in a scarlet red gown or another burning color, uncanny in the middle of a forest, wicker chairs and brave new love in a place that the maps forgot.

She counted bobby pins in the musty backroom of a pretty church, bells clanging something empty as she pricked herself with one.

"And then she fell into a million year slumber," Ava murmured.

"Hey Cinderella."

She startled, then smiled, gaze catching on Faye's reflection.

"Hey you."

Faye draped her arms over Ava's shoulders, pressing their cheeks together in the mirror.

"I haven't seen anything so wonderful since I met some awful little girl who stole the last cherry pop in the second grade, then tried to convince me that the cherry pop was made out of frozen blood anyway and that she should have it, since she was part of an elaborate coven of vampires."

Ava tossed her head back, the shaking in her hands halting for a millisecond before picking back up again.

"God, I really liked cherry," she said, "Sue me."

They both laughed something older and foreign, the ghosts of the girls they'd once been dissipating with every beat.

Faye squeezed her shoulder. "You're getting married, loser." A pause. "Scared?"

Ava glanced away, dropped her voice to a dramatic hush. "Terrified."

She was only half-kidding. But Faye didn't follow up with her usual eye-roll or parental lecture. She just smiled nervously, toyed with her own plain purple gown, darker than the rest for the Maid of Honor.

Ava frowned. "What's up?"

Faye hesitated for a second before whispering, "Promise you won't hate me?"

"Why would I – "

"Ava."

The voice cut into her - down to the bone.

The reaction Callum's presence brought out in Ava was always embarrassingly obvious. Her shoulders rose, her body perked like a serpent to song. Her heartbeat thrummed an old tune, blood clawing its way towards her flushed skin.

He stood there in a navy blue suit, black ink spiraling down his arms out from underneath his white dress shirt, rolled at the sleeves. No tie, black leather sneakers on, hair combed back the color of warm honey, dressed like he might have been if this were the wedding it was supposed to be.

His knuckles were still poised over the doorframe as if he'd been about to knock, but thought better of it.

Faye put her hands on Ava's shoulders, momentarily blocking Callum from her sight.

"Okay, listen. If you need to be mad at me for the rest of our lives, I understand. But Ava...you know how doubtful I was of him, of this. You've always known that. But the way you two have clung onto each other over the years defies everything that's ever made sense to me about love." Faye exhaled, hanging her head. "And I couldn't live with myself as your best friend if I hadn't made sure that you were sure."

Ava inhaled, glanced up at the ceiling, then back at Faye.

Faye paled. "Shit. I did the wrong thing."

Blinking back a tear, Ava shook her head, gripped Faye's arm.

They pressed their foreheads together, and she whispered, "Thank you." And then, "Give us a minute."

Faye nodded. In her peripheral vision, Ava saw her give Callum a passing smile on the way out the door before it shut.

The silence threatened to swallow them whole.

Callum was looking at everything but her - gaze raking over the fresh lilacs and pristine table runners, the makeup spilled behind her on the vanity, the toe of one ivory shoe.

But when he finally did look at her, she

understood why he hadn't. His features twisted with an emotion she'd never seen on him before - something melancholy and beautiful and tragic, like the window of a train with a beautiful view. Like a one-way ticket. Like knowing you could never go back home.

Callum rewove every thread and bead of her dress with his eyes, finally settling on her face. He cleared his throat, took another step towards her.

"Hey you."

Ava let out a laugh devoid of any humor, just a sharp, slanted sound.

He nodded at her wedding gown. "You going out somewhere?"

This laugh sounded more like a sob. She pressed her fingers to her forehead, her face to her palms.

"Why are you here?"

He raised a brow. "I was invited."

Her heart was racing, and it was getting hot in the cramped little room. "I didn't think you would come."

Callum's chuckle sounded pained, but there was a genuine smile on his face. "That's sweet."

Ava shot him a tired look, then continued counting bobby pins.

He took a step closer. "Hey."

"Don't."

Tears shielded Ava eyes, pooled before spilling across her cheeks, created jagged slants in her beautifully crafted makeup. Callum's lips were smooth against her forehead, persistent down the slope of her cheek. She didn't look at him – not when he was kissing her chin, not when he crouched down at her front, arms folded over her knees.

Callum's fingers wrapped around Ava's, dug into the white lace covering her lap.

She shook her head. They had Paris, they had New York – she finally opened her eyes to stare down at their intertwined fingers – but they didn't have this.

"Hey," Callum repeated, one hand curling under her chin. "I want to tell you something."

Ava blinked, drew in a ragged breath. Outside, she heard Faye standing guard by the door.

"This isn't fair," Ava said.

Callum nodded and whispered, "None of this was ever fair."

He let go of her hands to slip one of his into his suit jacket, surfacing with a familiar leather-bound book and a notecard taped to the face of it. Her mouth twitched.

"A wedding present," Callum explained, his grin broken. "I didn't want to show you at first. Thought you might try to make a run for it."

Through her tears, Ava smiled. "Smart move." She took the book, finger tracing the corners of the notecard, then the spine of the very thing that had brought them together. It didn't feel so sturdy anymore.

"This is the same…"

Callum nodded.

Ava exhaled another shaky breath, wiped at her cheeks. "How can I be crying over you this way, when I'm supposed to be marrying somebody else?"

Callum said nothing, just stared down at the book.

She slid her finger under the seam of the note's envelope, read what was inside.

"Because you and I were never a coincidence."

Ava frowned, held the card to her chest with one hand as the other finally flipped through the pages of the journal, only to come up blank every time. She turned and turned and turned, but not a speck of ink surfaced. She looked up at Callum, a question in her eyes.

"Riddle me this," Callum whispered, balancing himself with an arm on either side of her chair, thumbs brushing her thighs, a nervous tick. "A kid sees a beautiful girl on an airplane. And I'm talking, the most beautiful girl he's ever seen in his *life*. They have this moment, and then he's about to lose her. And he doesn't know anything other than that they're getting off this plane, she's with her mother, but he has to see her again. So he takes this ten euro journal he bought at de Gaulle that he knows she saw him with, writes his email inside the front cover, and drops it. Hopes that she's the kind of girl who would pick it up."

Ava braced herself on the chair, one hand over his. "And?"

Callum smiled. "And she was the kind of girl who picked it up." He reached up to cup her face, and she leaned into him. "Not kismet. Not coincidence. I was never chasing after this book. Day one, I was chasing after you."

"Why now?" Ava asked, pushing the book from her lap. He caught it in one hand. "Why right now? Why not before? Why couldn't this ever work then?"

"I just," Callum started, "know that neither of us have been given closure to anything in our lives. I wasn't going to be the one to leave you without letting you know what this was to me. I was wrong. I would fight for you forever. I'm going to find you in that version of the story. The one that *does* end with us."

Ava reached out to hold his face in her hands. "I *can't* say goodbye to you."

Callum straightened, pulled her hands from his face in one torturous movement. Walking backwards, he cleared his throat and ducked his head behind his arm so that she wouldn't see him cry.

He held onto the door before it swung open.

"Then…I'll see you in a minute, yeah?"

It was their favorite lie.

"Yeah," she whispered to his absence. "I'll see you in a minute."

A note from Callum:

This ends on an airplane.

Too many stories do.

They say that you're supposed to be with the girl who looks at you and makes you understand.

Every answer, every hidden star, every mystery etched underneath this horrible world sets alight, and you cannot return to ignorance because you'll never want to.

You're not supposed to be with the girl in whom you see yourself. You're supposed to be with the girl you see in everything else.

Ava is the whir of a jet, a screen fading to black, one-half the horizon and one-half the machine on fire flying towards it. If I'd thought the flight in was difficult, the flight home was lethal.

In the turbulence and empty seat across from mine, I kept waiting for a doctor to ask me what hurt. I kept waiting for Hades to hear me cry for Eurydice. But like we always understood, this isn't that kind of story.

Back at home, I'm sitting here, and there's no truth to excavate.

I've tasted life with her, I've endured life without

her. There's nothing beyond that.

A foolish man lets her remnants haunt him.

An even more foolish man holds on hope that she'll come back, doesn't keep the remains.

Which one am I?

Hold on.

There's a knock at the door.

ACKNOWLEDGEMENTS

A big thank you to my mother for tirelessly wading in my words with me. You have always been the woodwork behind my dreams.

And to my online family of beautiful creatives, every single one of you wonderful souls who have touched my work and I get to call friends – thank you for believing in my magic.

ABOUT THE AUTHOR

Naiche Lizzette Parker is a writer, witch, and lover of magic living in New York City. She was born with an abundance of words inside of her, and she's hoping to get them down on paper before her time is through.

Instagram: naichelizzette
Tumblr: crooked-queen.tumblr.com
Twitter: naichelizzette
Email: naichelizzetteparker@gmail.com
Website: naichelizzette.com

18957477R00091

Printed in Great Britain
by Amazon